BRINGING UP GIRLS
IN BOHEMIA

Michal Viewegh

BRINGING UP GIRLS IN BOHEMIA

translated from Czech by A.G. Brain

readers international

The title of this book in Czech is *Výchova dívek v Cechách,*
first published in 1994 by Ceský spisovatel in Prague.
Copyright 1994, Michal Viewegh and Ceský spisovatel.
Published by agreement with Wereldbibliotheek, Amsterdam.

First published in English by Readers International, Inc., USA,
and Readers International, London. Editorial inquiries to
RI London office at 8 Strathray Gardens, London NW3 4NY, UK.
US/Canadian inquiries to RI Book Service, P.O. Box 959,
Columbia, Louisiana 71418-0959 USA.

The editors gratefully acknowledge the support of the
National Endowment for the Arts, Washington DC.

Cover design by Jan Brychta.
Printed and bound in Malta

Library of Congress Catalog Card Number: 96-70319.
A catalog record for this book is held by the British Library.

ISBN 1-887378-05-7 Paperback

I

1. *The oddest thing of all, the thing that most strikes us when we embark on a story is the total void spreading out before us. The events have occurred and lie all around us in a continuous, formless mass without beginning or end. We can start anywhere...*
Vera Linhartova

When I returned from school that Wednesday with my daughter, the letter-box was literally full to bursting: apart from the usual *Lidové noviny*, it contained a large brown envelope with the page proofs of my novel plus a white envelope also addressed to me, and finally that controversial blue cellophane packet containing an advertising sample of a Procter and Gamble product. As I locked the letter-box, I noticed that the label with our name had been scored through with something sharp, most likely the key of some young enemy of all teachers.

The white envelope contained a brief letter from Kral, our local millionaire, offering me *a lucrative part-time job with easy hours.*

In other words, the beginning of *this* story did not lie in a formless mass in a total void, but in a white envelope in our letter-box on 16th June 1992.

"Anything in the mail?" my wife asked.

"I got the page proofs of my novel and an offer of a *lucrative job*," I said. "You got some sanitary towels."

My sincere compliments to Czech feminists.

I later read the letter more closely. I deduced that it was most likely a matter of coaching Agata, but I was rather perturbed that Kral clearly took it for granted, although he did not actually say as much, that I would accept his offer - and this could also be detected in the fact that he suggested only one date for me to meet him. I couldn't help recalling that famous line of Fitzgerald's: *The supercilious assumption was that on Sunday afternoon I had nothing better to do.*

"Do you intend to take it?" my wife asked.

Her intonation betrayed no hint of judgement as yet.

I shrugged.

"You were planning to write *a post-modern novel...*," she remarked with irony.

I was glad she said it because she might just as easily have said that we needed every penny we could get.

They were both equally true.

"We'll see," I said.

She went into the bathroom. I picked up the proofs and checked the first pages. I put the radio on loud in the background, as a result of which my wife later caught me performing an action I describe inexpertly as *the soul squirm.* She observed me condescendingly, her hair wrapped in a towel.

"OK," I admitted. "OK, I'm pleased with it."

"Good night," she announced in a matter-of-fact way.

Weariness with fabricated pictures of the world, suspicion of every myth - even (and clearly unjustly) of the time-honoured literary variety - grew so radically that it ushered in a peculiar era of reverence for the literature of fact and for the art and truth of the diary. Sergej Machonin.

2. I shall state straightaway that the following description of Kral's villa (and Kral's surname for that matter) is not entirely factual, because Kral's consent to the publication of this story was categorically conditional on my taking *certain precautions* to prevent any reliable identification. On the other hand, I should, of course, like to preserve the *genius loci* of that whole district and at least mention the fact that it is well out of earshot of Zbraslav's main street and that every third person passing by those ornamental wrought-iron fences on sandstone plinths behind which a generously proportioned lawn or the blue rim of a private swimming pool can be glimpsed here and there through the thick thuya hedge, is walking a thoroughbred dog on a self-retracting leash.

No sooner had I ascertained that the number in the letter tallied with the number on the gate-post at the front entrance than an unpleasant piercing noise could be heard as the automatic gate slid open. It was admittedly an entrance clearly intended for cars (the pedestrian entrance being to the right of it), but on looking round and seeing no car approaching, I assumed that I must have been spotted already by someone from behind the villa's darkened windows and that these gates, this villa, indeed this entire *world* was opening up all for me. And so, with an affable smile toward the villa's windows I stepped into the garden, and my left hand with fingers extended shot up in the air in a conventional gesture of thanks. (Yes, I know I can hear a gentle murmur break out among the reading public, but I hereby swear that I truly do not intend to construct the entire novel around that gratuitous gesture, not even if, in so doing, I might ensure my immortality.) The next moment however - and I'm still unable to explain it - I was nearly run down by a black Volkswagen Golf convertible. I instinctively leapt out of the way as soon as I heard the characteristic crunch of tires on gravel. The car missed me by swerving slightly - in the process of which the kerbside wheels went up onto the grass - and then halted for a moment a short distance away. Although the day was very warm the roof wasn't down, and it was hard to see inside through the dark, tinted rear window - but for a split second I did catch sight of Beata's pale, engrossed and almost severe face in the rear-view mirror: the lips tightly pursed and the eyes concealed behind sunglasses. She assured herself that I was still alive, put the car into gear and disappeared behind the villa.

The wheels actually raised the dust slightly.

Immediately afterwards, before I had even had time to collect my thoughts, an unknown assailant knocked me to the ground from behind and twisted my arms up my back. I yelped in astonishment and pain.

7

"Don't you ever try that on us again!"

The owner of the voice dug his knee with force into my kidneys.

" 'Cos we're not stupid!"

"Ow!"

"Or maybe you think we are?"

"For God's sake! Ow!!"

The voice laughed and was joined by another one. They were young male voices.

"OK, pal - looking for someone?"

There was no let-up in the knee pressure. I had never before examined a blade of grass from so close. I tried to raise my head in order to reply, but they pushed it back down. With effort I took several breaths and managed to mumble my name into the turf.

"Never heard of him," the voice said mockingly.

My initial fright gave way to outrage.

"At half past five," I ejaculated furiously, "I have a meeting with Mr Kral. An *appointment.*"

I would never have believed that so few words could require so much effort.

"Oh yeah?" said the voice doubtfully. The pressure vanished from my kidneys and my hands were freed. "So why didn't you ring the bell in the *usual* way?"

They helped me up nonetheless. Both of them had ties, and both of them were on the larger side. I dusted myself off with annoyance.

"Well, sorry about that then," said the other one with a grin.

His voice betrayed not the slightest regret. He looked me over with interest.

"So you're the *next* one?"

I didn't grasp his meaning.

"What do you mean, the *next* one?"

They briefly exchanged glances.

They escorted me to a marble staircase that led up to a spacious summer terrace, equipped rather intriguingly with two white plastic tables, four purple plastic mini-armchairs and one orange and green parasol. They motioned me to take a seat there.

"Good luck then," said the blonde one.

"And next time - *the bell*, remember," said the other.

I seethed in silence. They departed merrily.

I mounted the staircase to the terrace - with a certain forced dignity in my gait - but I hesitated over which of the tables to sit at, since one was swimming in spilt milkshake of some kind while the other was piled high with a bizarre collection of dirty cups, glossy magazines, skin creams, hair clips and pink aerobic dumb-bells. Crowning the entire still-life, however, was a sturdy Braun hair drier that lay there *switched on*, quietly humming to itself while wafting the pages of the fashion magazine *Tina*. An extension cord ran back through the open door into the murky depths of the front hall.

"Hi there!" Kral boomed out from inside, but I couldn't see him in that darkness.

"Good morning," I called nonetheless.

"Take a seat. I'll be right with you!"

He could be heard going upstairs somewhere. Suddenly a door banged and there was the sound of muffled voices - his and a girl's. I picked up the hair drier and used it to blow crumbs off the table. The English garden below me looked a trifle unkempt: the shrubs were unpruned, the lawn long in need of mowing, the rosebeds un-weeded, and the white gravel on the front path was overgrown with dandelions and other weeds. In addition, certain gardening jobs - such as the repair of the low stone wall or the trimming of the front hedge - had been badly botched.

"Hi there!" Kral said breathlessly. "I'm glad you came."

He was a good-looking man but gave an impression of weari-ness (one which I was never able to dispel afterwards). Agata sim-pered behind him:

"Good morning!"

She performed a mocking parody of a curtsy and grabbed a handful of potato chips, knocking over a glass of Coca-Cola in the process.

"Hi there!" I said in the local fashion.

For some reason unknown to myself she burst out laughing. A few little chips landed on the sleeve of my light-coloured jacket.

"Agata!" Kral admonished her mildly.

"Sorry," she said. She kicked off her clogs and in quick succession performed a series of gymnastic exercises known as the cartwheel and the splits. Then she put her clogs back on.

"Wouldn't you like a Coke?" she said politely. "Or chips?"

"Let's go into my office," Kral suggested.

I knew he had bought the villa in 1990, but the fact he had not lived there long could also be detected from the way he pronounced the words *my office*.

It did not escape my attention that it was locked - which no doubt explained its tidiness: everything was in order on the stained-oak desk, the files were arranged neatly on the shelves, the honey-coloured carpet was carefully vacuumed, and there was no freshly spilt milkshake on the executive chair made of wood and real leather. Dominating the room was the noble curve of an imposing gold table lamp. I have to admit that (in spite of a certain lack of originality) the luxurious elegance of the office impressed me.

"You have a nice place here," I said sincerely.

This clearly pleased him. He poured scotch into two glasses and then, a trifle ostentatiously, opened the door of the built-in fridge and brought a glassful of ice cubes. He sat down opposite me.

"I read that book of yours... *Views on a Murder*?"

"That's right."

"I liked it."

Nice office, nice book.

"Thanks."

"My daughter does a bit of writing, too."

"Really?"

"It might assist her self-awareness," he remarked pensively. He was staring at the desk top. When he raised his eyes to me, I realised from his expression that he had apparently intended it as a question.

10

"Of course," I said. "Definitely."

He nodded in agreement. He seemed to me to liven up.

"To tell you the truth that's something she could do with a bit of," he said. "Self-awareness, I mean. She's going through a *difficult patch* at the moment."

"I'd say it's fairly normal." I chuckled: "She's good at gymnastics..."

He stared at me in astonishment.

Something jarred.

But of course - it was Beata he had in mind.

Naturally, I was somewhat taken aback - and Kral, being a businessman to his fingertips, seized on my hesitation.

"So," he said briskly. "What about a *creative writing course*?"

"Well..."

"Let's get down to brass tacks: You would come here four times a week, Monday to Thursday, for two hours a day, let's say. We are generally away for the weekend, so you'll have Fridays, Saturdays and Sundays off, of course."

As a Czech teacher through and through, I couldn't help noticing the switch from the conditional to future tense.

"But that's an awful lot of time, eight hours a week," I said hesitantly. "At this very moment I have the page proofs of a novel on my desk, and I don't know whether..."

"Two hours a day? Do you know how many hours I work a day? - Twelve. Fifteen sometimes."

He stood up and went to sit at his desk.

"After all, we're not talking about boring old *coaching*... The program will be entirely up to you. You can more or less do what you like. And nobody's going to insist you have to stay here at home to do your chatting about books..."

He kept his eyes fixed on me until I finally nodded.

There was *change* in the air.

Impending change, regardless of the eventual outcome, has always aroused in me an irrational feeling of joyful anticipation.

"Which brings us to the question of payment," Kral said. Pushing himself away from the desk in his castor-bottomed chair,

11

he reached out quite far for a *notebook* which, while swivelling back, he opened, switched on and placed lightly on the desk, the fingers of his right hand coming to rest on the small keyboard. It struck me that there was something definitely *choreographic* about his movements.

"How much would you have in mind?"

I couldn't help blushing slightly. According to the *Decree of the Government of the Czech Republic on payment conditions of budgetary employees and certain other organisations, dated 22 April 1992,* my gross monthly salary at the time amounted to 3,680 crowns, and on the ladder of fifty select occupations published in the daily press, teachers' pay was at rung forty-nine.

"Do you have any particular idea?" Kral repeated affably.

"No."

"This is what I suggest then: eight thousand a month cash in hand - plus, where appropriate, something along the lines of a *productivity bonus*."

He really shouldn't do that to me, I said to myself miserably. It isn't fair.

"Is it a deal?" said Kral.

Coming on top of all those declarative sentences, I valued the fact that this was a quite straightforward question.

I pulled myself together and asked for three days to think it over.

That was something he hadn't expected.

"All right," he agreed sulkily.

3. I wasn't feeling in the best of spirits either. I kept on harking back in my mind both to our conversation and to the letter referred to earlier, and it became clearer and clearer to me just how firmly and cockily convinced Kral had been - and apparently still was - that for eight thousand a month a young Czech teacher and writer would immediately drop everything and spend four evenings every week sitting over the naïve literary efforts of his older daughter. In a sense it was very insulting. I decided that the very next day I would devote myself entirely to mustering my professional pride.

The task was not a particularly easy one, however - after all, if your only novel still happens to be at the page proof stage and the Principal of your school happens to be an individual whose supreme intellectual achievement is a 25-year-old thesis entitled *Physical training equipment for boy and girl pupils*, then your professional pride is fairly well submerged.

"Good morning," I said, on entering the office.

"Good morning to you," said my colleague and friend Jaromir Nadany, a man of mature years.

He seemed to be in a good mood, which wasn't always the case. (I tried to have an understanding for the vagaries of his moods - and my degree of success usually depended on how well I was able to conjure up what it must be like for him to spend days and weeks on end cooped up in a tiny house with no other company than a black cat. *My last cat*, Jaromir would sometimes say.)

"Oh, good morning," said my colleague Irenka.

"Good morning," said my colleague Liba.

"Good morning, good morning!" my colleague Lenka said.

Colleague Chvatalova-Sukova said nothing. In lieu of a greeting, she gave me the sort of look a driver gives a squashed hedgehog. Her face then resumed its former worried expression, and she continued rummaging through the office cupboards. At length she stood up:

"Lenicka! Libuska! Irenka!" she exclaimed in her own version of Macha's famous trinity. "You don't happen to have an empty coffee jar by any chance?"

"No."

"We've already given you all our coffee jars, Miluska dear," Irenka explained.

A look of utter despair came into Miluska's eyes which suggested strongly that the Principal was going off fishing later that morning, if not straightaway. Jaromir took pity on her; he tipped his instant coffee into a polythene lunch bag and mutely handed her the empty jar.

"Little ones are a waste of time," Chvatalova-Sukova commented, suppressing her satisfaction, and rushed out to the school garden with the glass jar and a U.S. Army trenching tool. As always, she moved her limbs in time with an inaudible composition playing somewhere beneath the dome of her skull.

We went out of the office into the corridor and crowded round the window. Miluska was hovering in the dewy grass.

"Ode to Joy," Lenka surmised now that our lady colleague was digging purposefully in the flower bed. Her face reliably betrayed every worm found. Unpromising flowerbeds were immediately abandoned by Miluska with an expression of mute reproach. It must be said that she moved with great alacrity.

"The Flight of the Bumble-Bee," said Liba.

By now the familiar morning din rose from the cloakrooms below. Agata was among the first arrivals, unfortunately. The moment she saw me her face lit up:

"Good morning!" she called with exaggerated emphasis.

"Hi," I said with reserve. I tried to follow my colleagues through the office door, but Agata almost blocked my path. A starched lace chemise was poking out from beneath her black T-shirt. She smiled affably, her eyes well fixed on my face.

"Well?" she asked good-naturedly. Almost *matronly*, in fact.

"No comment. Your shirt-tail's showing."

She looked at me as if it was the funniest thing she'd ever heard.

"That's how they're worn," she eventually said with authority. Then she twirled the rucksack with her school books around and flung it along the corridor in the direction of her classroom.

"Well done," I said rather wearily by now. "Is there something you need?"

"Me?" Amazement in her innocent eyes. "No..."

"So move further down the tram," I said, although I tended to avoid droll sayings of that variety.

When we don't know what to do with them, we herd them into the classroom.

"Dad sends his regards," Agata said huffily.

I could feel the eyes of my female colleagues on the back of my neck.

"Thank you."

I quickly shut the door.

"Going into *business*?" Irenka said.

An aside inspired by worms:

When Chvatalova-Sukova came upon a particularly large specimen, she would occasionally tear it in half in her eagerness to extract it from the ground. There is a lesson to be learnt here, because this true story - in which, by sheer chance, I became a direct participant (and perhaps yet again only a writer can appreciate the good fortune of an author who, at a moment of total disbelief in invented worlds is handed by fate an *authentic event*) - is, in a certain sense, no more than a *fat worm*. If I want to get it out whole, I will have to proceed with the utmost caution.

Incidentally: the trenching tool that Chvatalova-Sukova always uses to obtain bait is no ordinary trenching tool. Similarly, the jeep, which from the spring onwards stands in front of the school on schooldays is no ordinary all-terrain vehicle. Were I now to say that the jeep and the trenching tool once formed part of the equipment of the U.S. Army, my statement would run the risk of being regarded as the preposterous invention of an unbridled spinner of yarns - so I had better quote in full an article published under the title "Good Idea" in the *Zbraslav News* (issue 4, 1992, page 3):

Last month the enterprising spirit of the Principal of Zbraslav's Vladislav Vancura Elementary School scored another success. He was the first elementary school principal in Prague 5 to react to the U.S. Embassy's announcement of the opportunity to buy up cheaply the stock and equipment being left behind in Germany by a departing contingent of the U.S. Army. In this way our school obtained at very low cost (the goods being exempt from import duty and all tax, including VAT and gift tax) eight extending ladders usable as wall-bars, gun tripods that will find use as easels for the much needed portable blackboards, a set of working boots and clothes and, last but not least, a second-hand jeep.   Yet further proof that it's better to do a deal than hold out a begging bowl... Congratulations!

At precisely eight o'clock the second bell rang. Miluska was still not back.

"Oh, shut up!" Lenka snapped at the bell.

"Already?" Liba sighed.

"There's no greater adventure than the search for knowledge," declared colleague Jaromir.

However, the roar of a jeep starting up beneath the office window suddenly announced that a trip to Orlik was rather more of an adventure. We took a cautious look out of the window: the Principal, Mr Naskocil, in his favourite working uniform with the name Sergeant L. Wright (which for some reason he refused to remove) had just given the final orders to the two lads on the back of the jeep: Havlicek, whose by now rather protracted task was to initiate the Principal into the niceties of operating a personal computer (apparently in the short intervals between casts) and Laznovsky, who was at present holding the fishing rods and the blue kit-bag (somewhere in the depths of which Miluska's worms were no doubt squirming in Jaromir's coffee jar).

"Why Laznovsky?" I enquired.

"No one," Liba informed me, "beats him at cleaning eel slime off a landing net."

"Oh, I see."

"Apart from Miluska, naturally."

According to the surviving time-table for that year, my first period on a Friday morning was composition with 8C, whose teacher I had also been for four years already. (Just briefly about my class: some of the pupils were, to put it simply, a trifle *difficult*, and it had taken me a long time to build up a relationship with them - although even in the years when we were getting on fairly well together, the entire class would occasionally fall prey to a sort of collective lunacy in the course of which they would mostly toss about and crush underfoot several boxes of coloured chalks, or use an over-ripe orange to create an original pattern on the newly painted walls - and then, on my furious entry, would merely stare at the floor, still sweaty and out of breath, and when I'd go round angrily lifting their chins to look them in the face, their eyes would display nothing but childish innocence.) But to return to composition - I naturally *burst with enthusiasm and overflowed with ideas. Moreover, the incredible range and abundance of the exercises which I prepared never ceased to provide the astounded pupils with evidence of their mother tongue as an effective tool of self-knowledge...* In other words: the inevitable price to be paid for writing in the first person is the impossibility of describing *truthfully* any successful lessons one might have had.

"Replace the verb in the following sentences with a suitable interjection," Marcela read out the instructions for the next exercise. Example: The frog *jumped* into the water. - The frog went plop into the water."

"This is almost embarrassingly easy," I said. "So let's get it over with quickly. Radek, you start."

"The balloon *burst*," Radek Zeleny read out and thought for a moment. "The balloon *went plop*."

The schoolboy howler. Even the least arrogant of intellectuals will give a little smile of sympathy (although *Prague* intellectuals will most likely pretend politely that they heard nothing - such as when, in their presence some poor benighted ignoramus unintentionally garbles the name of Jorge Luis Borges). I'm under no illusion: just one more schoolboy howler and I'll never rid myself of the *superficial humorist* label.

During that morning, my pupil-to-be was evoked indirectly on two further occasions.

First during break, when, as part of *pedagogical surveillance* I was aimlessly wandering the corridor and I discovered on one of the notice boards an old sketch of Beata's dating from the period when she was in 8th year. It was an accomplished charcoal drawing, the sole subject of which was a left hand - her own, no doubt. It struck me that the image of that girl was being presented to me bit by bit, like the picture question in some TV quiz; so far I knew only the reflection of her face in the rear-view mirror and a six-year-old sketch of her left hand - and I suddenly realised that I was being overcome by a sort of stupid curiosity.

And at one-thirty Kral was waiting in front of the school.

4. He was sitting in his turquoise Audi. I knew the driver: it was one of his bodyguards. Agata was sitting in the back and fielding the comments of her fellow pupils, who were thronging around her.

He came to meet me with a smile.

"Hi there. On your way home? We'll drop you off..."

I nodded in the direction of the school canteen:

"I'm just off to lunch."

"We're going to lunch, too."

I said nothing.

"What's for lunch?"

"Boiled beef in tomato sauce," one of the young lads coming from lunch told him.

"Oh, yuck," Agata said from inside the car. "Yu-u-uck!"

Her imitation of vomiting was unpleasantly accurate.

"Agata," Kral admonished her with a loving smile before turning back to me: "Listen! How about having lunch with us?"

"But I like tomato sauce," I said cheerfully.

For the first time in my life I realise how a secretary must feel when her boss invites her out to lunch.

"Forget the tomato sauce."

He gave me a friendly smile.

"For the first time in my life I realise how a secretary must feel when her boss invites her out to lunch..."

The driver leaned out of his seat slightly:

"Oh yeah? How?"

The corners of his mouth twitched in anticipation of a juicy quip. His transformation into my buddy was a bit too abrupt for my liking.

"Dreadful," I said.

"Oh yeah. I see what you mean," he said disappointedly.

"But that's something else entirely!" Kral protested, although I'd happily wager that he was actually flattered by the analogy.

"*Really*?"

He looked me straight in the eye:

"Of course it is."

I threw up my hands:

"OK then."

I joined Agata in the back of the car.

"Tomato sauce, yu-u-uck," she went again.

"Yu-u-uck," went Kral.

"Yu-u-uck," went the driver.

And off we drove.

We were travelling fairly slowly, as if they wanted to give me ample time to appreciate the noiseless power of the engine, the flawless suspension, the velvety soft upholstery of the interior and the pleasantly cool air-conditioning. However, it seems I was insufficiently overawed for Kral's liking, as he felt it necessary to give me an additional demonstration of his mobile phone: in feigned impatience he urgently dialled a number, but since there was no reply, he had to make do with calling his wife to let her know he was bringing home a guest with him.

"Set an extra place," he requested affably. However, Mrs Kralova's (highly audible) reaction - first uncomprehending and then a trifle brusque - was fairly eloquent evidence of the pointlessness of his call at a moment when scarcely two hundred yards separated us from the dining room in their villa.

Kral and I lunched alone, Agata and the driver having disappeared somewhere. Similarly there was no sign of Beata. Since Kral did not feel any need to comment on her absence, however, I did not even ask. It must be admitted that two aperitifs did a lot to relax me, but I was still a bit wary. After the soup Kral went out for a moment, and I spent the time looking out of the dining room window at the rest of the garden. Here too a number of oddities caught my eye: the stumps of amateurishly pruned shrubs, overgrown flowerbeds that had sunk into the ground, gooseberry and blackcurrant bushes whose roots were totally uncovered. What crowned it all, however, were the ruins of a compost bin heaped up with an incredible hotchpotch of branches, earth, cardboard boxes, stones and wire.

"Your gardener is a butcher," I told Kral on his return.

"Jokes like that," he said with unexpected animosity, "don't go down well with me."

I didn't understand:

"I don't understand..."

"I don't know who's been telling you stories," he said icily, "but I'd leave it at that, if I were you."

"I only meant to say that the garden..."

He silenced me with a look. A nasty look. Just what's going on here? I asked myself.

The tension was unbearable.

"Fine," I said.

I chose my words with care:

"If I've offended you in any way, I'm sorry."

He nodded magnanimously. Who the hell did he think he was? I couldn't resist taking him to task slightly:

"I'll therefore keep my opinions on the garden to myself and restrict my comments to a number of *purely pedagogical* matters," I said forcefully. "Firstly, I *also* wait for my daughter in front of the school even though most of her friends have been going home on their own for a long time already, so I'd be the last one to criticise this sort of paternal caution, but to wait for her in a luxury limousine is utterly stupid. Even without that you don't make things easy for her, so that palace on wheels just makes things worse. And secondly, a *generous* father is no doubt an entirely admirable figure, but your utterly limitless tolerance and uncritical adoration will provoke the same problems which - in my view - you are possibly having with Beata at present."

I gave a short gasp.

He regarded me pensively. Is he going to throw me out? I wondered.

"It could be that I'm too *soft*," he reflected with surprising equanimity.

He looked out the window. There was clearly something on his mind.

"She can't walk there on her own, though. Get one thing straight: when you've got a bit of money, people are just a bit envious of you. - But when you're *really* rich, you unfortunately have *real* enemies."

"I can imagine," I said in a conciliatory tone.

"Listen," he said very quietly all of a sudden. "Take the job."

And I replied:
"All right, then."

II

1. Of itself, the fact that Beata *did a bit of writing* did not particularly surprise me: after all, it's a well-known fact that each of us *is pained by the thought of disappearing, unheard and unseen, into an indifferent universe* and this is proved by the *irresistible proliferation of graphomania among politicians, taxi drivers, childbearers, lovers, murderers, thieves, prostitutes, officials, doctors and patients.* (Milan Kundera). Moreover, I knew she had already spent a year at the arts faculty (although after passing her exams at the end of the summer term she had interrupted her studies *at her own request*), an environment - as I myself had the opportunity to discover - in which one *justifies oneself* through writing; not to write at all immediately arouses suspicions that one has got to university through nepotism. So far so good, therefore. What I couldn't make out, however, was why Beata's writing was so important to Kral, and his insistence on a creative writing course made no sense to me. Would he court a violin teacher in the same way? I asked myself.

"So what's expected of you, then?" my wife quizzed me as I was getting ready to go on duty for the first time that Sunday evening. In spite of my protests, my daughter wrapped me up three curd-cheese buns for the journey.

"That's the question I ask myself," I replied absentmindedly, because I was just wondering what I ought to take with me: A red marking-pen? A photo of Hemingway? "I'm supposed to teach her to write... He's expecting *a miracle* in other words."

"A miracle, eh? So you're planning to *charm* her?"

In spite of her mocking expression she looked a trifle doubtful.

"I'm not *planning* to charm her," I declared with mock primness. "I happen to charm young girls *unwittingly*."

22

"Ha ha ha," my daughter said disapprovingly as she had no liking at all for even the most innocent comments on that particular theme. She had not yet reached her ninth birthday at the beginning of that summer.

My wife remained silent. Admittedly Kral's lucrative offer had turned me into an *exceptionally capable and respectable man* as far as Friday night and the whole of Saturday were concerned; but now Sunday was come. It was not hard to guess what form of eventual *drain on profits* was playing on her mind.

"How many times will you go there?" my daughter asked.

"Many times."

I turned to my wife:

"Many times, because *poverty, that mangy bitch, already sprawls across our threshold...*"

"Is it true we're poor?" my daughter asked with genuine interest.

"Have you ever seen a rich teacher?" my wife said.

I kissed her:

"But you *will*, though."

As soon as I arrived at the entrance to Kral's villa, the sliding gate again opened noisily. I stayed where I was.

The two giants stood in the garden, beckoning to me with the remote control.

"Hi there, teacher man!"

"Hi, boys!"

"Come on, then!"

"No chance!" I said resolutely.

"Come on, don't be frightened," they laughed.

I did not budge an inch. They reviled me merrily.

The one who had been driving Kral's Audi on Thursday eventually came to let me in. I noticed that his eyes were red and puffy.

"Something went wrong with that lock again," he explained. He offered me his hand: "The name's Petr. They call me Petrik."

I nodded towards the spot where they had knocked me down last time:

"I believe I've already introduced myself."

A short laugh escaped from him.

"You're not intending to thump me today?" I enquired.

The other one arrived.

"He wants to know if we're going to thump him today..." Petrik cheerfully informed him.

"Not today," the other one laughed. He said his name was Jirka but everyone called him Jirik. His eyes were in a worse way than Petrik's.

"Who have you been mourning?" I asked. "Arnold Schwarzenegger hasn't died, has he?"

It transpired that the two fellows had been competing to see who could last longer being shut in a car with tear-gas sprayed inside. Jirik had won.

Kral leaned over from the terrace:

"Come on in!" he called and disappeared once more.

"Run along, then," they dismissed me.

"What about the body search?"

"Run along," they said, pushing me. "He's rushing off to tennis."

"I'm amazed at your casualness. What if I had Semtex in my blackboard pointer?" They brayed with laughter. Jirik managed to sneeze some mucous onto his jacket.

Well at least I've got *those* idiots off my back, I hope, I thought to myself.

Rather naïvely I was expecting that my first day of duty would assume if not a *ceremonial*, then at least an *official* character - but in the event my anticipated *induction* (if one may at all describe it thus in this case) took place rather hurriedly and without much dignity; Kral was hastily changing for tennis, and he imparted all the instructions to me as he moved between bedroom and bathroom.

"Beata's in her room - I told her you'd be starting at six. It's gone half past already. My wife will make you coffee in the kitchen."

He kicked off the underpants he had been wearing and dashed off naked to the bathroom. He left the door wide open. I noted that my rooted aversion to self-assured naked men had actually intensified since my conscript days.

"Tell her I insist you have to stay at home for the first sessions - just in case she wanted to go off somewhere..."

"Fine."

"I will easily be back in two hours. If I don't make it, hang around for me."

It sounded harsh, as if all the affability had been exhausted in the course of our two earlier meetings.

"Fine."

He put on a green-and-white polo shirt. At last he looked in my direction:

"As I was telling you: she's having a *creative crisis*. You're not going to find it easy. Don't be put off."

He pulled on a pair of white Adidas socks - each of which bore three green stripes:

"I should have been on the court long ago."

I couldn't help thinking that the rush suited him. All those curt instructions merely concealed a lack of self-confidence. That was something else I used to see during my army days.

"Civic Democratic Open Cup?" I asked jokingly.

"That's not until December. In the sports hall," he explained. He smiled superciliously. "Today I'm playing Petr Cermak."

One ought not, however, interpret the active nature of the poet's speech as meaning that poetry uses words to create a new, autonomous and artificial reality as is sometimes mistakenly maintained. There truly is only one reality. Jan Mukarovsky, *Study in Poetics.*

I sat all alone in the kitchen for several long minutes. Then Mrs Kralova came in:

"With or without milk?" she asked curtly - she had clearly received her instructions, too. I felt like a TV repairman.

"Without, please."

"How can you drink it black?" she said reproachfully. She had made herself a *white* one.

I shrugged apologetically and offered her a bun - the fact that I had brought three curd-cheese buns with me unexpectedly cheered her up. She started to ask me about my daughter: Had she wrapped them herself? All by herself? What had she said while doing it? Whose idea had it been really? Had it *really* been hers?

I am used to such questions from both my grandmothers, so I'm able to reply to them - if this doesn't sound too conceited - without all the usual ageist angst. Naturally it helped improve my relationship with Mrs Kralova.

"A little angel," she eventually said with genuine emotion.

She sighed.

There could be no doubt that her mind was now elsewhere.

She pointed towards the ceiling:

"I'll tell you one thing - she's almost twenty. She ought to be at work," she said seriously. "And for another thing, she ought to get married."

Any further opinions about what twenty-year-old girls ought to do were suddenly interrupted by the arrival of thirteen-year-old Agata. She had a lollipop in her mouth.

"Hey," she said, with a delighted smack of the lips but no greeting. "Are you here already?"

"Yes. I'm already here."

"Would you mind saying good evening?" said Mrs Kralova. "And take off those shoes."

Agata kicked her plimsolls off into a corner and stuck the lollipop on the coloured supplement that was lying on the table in front of me. Then she walked over to the fridge in her bare feet, following the pattern on the tiles. She pulled a plastic bottle of Coca-Cola out of the fridge and an enormous tomato which she stuffed whole into her mouth - as could be expected, juice filled with yellow pips started to ooze out of both corners of her mouth.

"Agata!" said Mrs Kralova.

Agata giggled, lost her breath and started to choke - red in the face and with horribly goggling eyes she came and fell at my feet with eloquent gestures; I obediently thumped her scrawny back several times with the flat of my hand. At last she caught her breath:

26

"Thanks muchly."

Her eyes were brimming with tears.

"That's more than I can stand," said Mrs Kralova. As she left the kitchen, she cast a sad glance in my direction.

"What's bitten her now?" Agata said reproachfully.

I couldn't help smiling, though I knew she would take my *teacher's* smile to mean approval, or encouragement even.

This was confirmed straightaway:

"How do you get on with Beata?" I asked. She was just doing some sort of stretching exercises.

"Which nails?" she said without interest, feigning deafness.

I patiently repeated my question.

She stared at me in scornful amazement.

"How am I supposed to get on with her when she's not been talking to me for the past week?"

"She doesn't *talk* to you?"

"She doesn't talk to *anyone*...," she protested.

God help me, I thought to myself.

"Why isn't she talking?"

She obviously wanted to say something, but in the end she just grimaced:

"Because she's a cow."

2. When, a few minutes after six o'clock, I was walking up the marble staircase to Beata's attic room, I noticed I had a slight attack of butterflies. (It surprised me somewhat; when I was starting out as a teacher, I admittedly suffered from butterflies on a couple of occasions - as everyone did, I expect - but by then I could enter any sort of classroom twenty-six times a week without it ever occurring to me to be nervous.) The staircase emerged onto a sunny mezzanine with a small conservatory where someone had created a very cosy corner with the help of three wicker armchairs, a coffee table and a charming table lamp with a pink silk-tasselled lampshade. *All it needs is a coffee pot and two cups - and the quiet chat about literature can commence,* I said to myself. On the door of Beata's boudoir was a large rectangular label with the word PRIVATE in English as well as a dozen or so old stickers with the portraits of various bands, while the numerous score-marks on many of them were evidence of vain attempts to scrape them off. When, after my third round of knocking, I received no audible response, I entered the room with the words *May I come in?*

The room was filled with a dim and oppressive twilight as the brocade curtains admitted the least possible light. So it took me a moment to find my bearings: the entire room was divided in two by a long bookcase about five feet high that ran from the opposite wall and ended directly in front of the door after the fashion of a ship's prow by the addition of a figurehead in the shape of a mermaid, whose expressively upraised arms served as a coat stand. In the smaller part of the room was a plain study area with a desk heaped up with books and paper. The remaining two thirds of the room was dominated by an original corner seating *assemblage* comprising two amorphous piles of sausage-shaped cushions, two low rickety leather poufs and one authentic dentist's chair. The role of the traditional coffee table was assumed by half a Texaco oil barrel standing in the middle of an oriental-patterned rug. In the corners of the room hung large black loudspeakers, and between the darkened windows hung a polystyrene board covered with hand-written notes and cuttings from *Vokno* review. The covers on the unmade bed, on which Beata lay facing the wall, however, were sadly conventional.

"Hi, there. So I'm here. Put another way: into your cosy - and, incidentally, very original - student room, steps *pure, unadulterated art.*"

No reaction. I once more scanned the entire interior.

"OK : *Bourgeois* art, then."

Nothing.

"It can't be helped," I said, " - seeing that you failed to run me over..."

The fair hair on the pillow did not budge an iota. Maybe she's deaf, it struck me. But they'd have told me, for heaven's sake. I pondered for a moment on the best place to sit, and at last sat down cautiously on the pile of aforementioned sausage-shaped cushions, only to discover to my horror the very next moment, that they were filled with water: the soft material immediately took possession of my centre of gravity and washed smoothly from side to side several times before forcing me into the pose of Goya's *Naked Maja*.

"This is a swamp, not an armchair..."

My first attempt at getting free landed me in the *Death of Marat* pose. The silence was broken solely by my own huffing and puffing. I was second time lucky. I perched on the wooden edge of the dentist's chair:

"All right, then: joking aside."

I reflected for a moment.

"Let's level with each other. Your father was telling me that you do a bit of writing, and he asked me if I'd be willing to talk to you about it a couple of times a week. I explained to him that I really don't have any time to spare and that in addition I'm a trifle sceptical about such courses. The reason I eventually accepted his proposal was above all because he offered me - at least from my perspective - lots of money."

It seemed to me as if she had *nodded*.

"At the same time, though, I couldn't help feeling that for some reason or other your writing means a great deal to him. Admittedly he told me that it was your *secret wish* to have a course on literary style but frankly, for the past three minutes I have been having doubts about how well informed he actually is about his elder daughter's secret wishes..."

She remained silent. Her head rested motionless on the pillow. Apart from that plethora of fair hair I had not obtained any additional pieces to my jigsaw.

"Do you want me to leave?" I asked.

No reply.

"Because I refuse to force anyone to do anything..."

Nothing.

"I'm going. I'll do without the money. I'll simply go on having meatloaf for Sunday dinner. In fact I love meatloaf."

And tomato sauce, I recalled.

"The loafer leaves," I said, chiefly for my own benefit.

Nonetheless, the absence of any reaction at all from her made me more than a little nervous. I remembered Kral and his *don't be put off.* I leaned over towards her hair (in what is known as a *forward-bent pedagogical offensive*):

"Listen, Beata," I said with a certain degree of urgency, "I'm nine years married - and if there's one thing I *really can't stand* it's *tawdry theatrical scenes* like this one. What if we simply draw back those curtains, let a little light and fresh air in here for a change and try to have a calm and non-committal chat? Alternatively," - I was fired with a sudden idea - "how about us simply abandoning this impressive combination of dental office and crude-oil dump and transferring for a moment to those nice, optimistic wicker armchairs down there on the mezzanine?"

Someone entered. I squinted in irritation at the oblong of light.

"Am I disturbing you?" Agata politely enquired. "Why are you sitting here in the dark?"

"Yes, you are!" I raised my voice for the first time in that house. "Sorry, but you are to leave us alone!"

Affronted, she tossed her hair and slammed the door behind her.

"I overheard your reply," I told Beata, as affably as I could.

Water off a duck's back.

"Beata, please." By now my patient manner with her was demanding not a little effort. "Couldn't we just *have a go*? Couldn't we simply try to accommodate your father? Let's just see - it might even be worth it..."

And I went on to add:

"We're not talking about *coaching*, for heaven's sake - so why make things difficult for each other?"

And also:

"All that's needed is a tiny bit of goodwill on your part."

Not to mention:

"I promise you we'll not use a *single* exercise book..."

I even tried - under the influence of films set in psychiatric clinics - to provoke her:

"You've got a tendency to greasy hair - have you noticed?"

She lay like a corpse.

30

Giving up, I went back to the dentist's chair.

"Jesus Christ," I sighed aloud, "this is going to be hard-earned cash and no mistake."

She raised herself on her elbows and turned towards me a face of stone:

"You can say that again!" she hissed with unconcealed apathy.

So that's what I'm doing.

All of a sudden she started to be poorly and ill, coughing and pining and wasting away, growing paler and thinner, grieving and sighing. Karel Capek, *The Princess of Soliman.*

I must admit that Beata's sudden outburst stunned me for a good few minutes: incapable of saying anything coherent or sensible, I mutely scanned the murky room.

It took a feeling of umbrage - that I had manipulated myself into with a bit of necessary hypocrisy (*Who does that girl think she is?*) - for me to pull myself together somewhat; after all, I'm no *Zen buddhist* to spend an hour and a half in the half-dark just with my own (hardly inspiring) thoughts.

It'll make a great *story*, I consoled myself wearily.

"Hey," I said, "can't we put the radio on, at least?"

I was more or less resigned to the fact that every one of my remarks would be lost without trace in that tenebrous space.

"Or the cassette player? It's true that silence is an effective remedy, but it's not a good idea to have an *overdose* at the outset... What if I go and make a milkshake - like the one I sat in on your terrace last Thursday? It was really nice - I licked it off my crotch when I got home."

This time she couldn't help an audible titter. It only made the subsequent silence more dogged.

I'll still get you, you so-and-so, I said to myself, but I was running out of ideas.

"Or what if I vacuumed the place?" I suggested at a quarter to seven.

At seven o'clock I said:

31

"The only reason I asked was to keep the conversation from flagging..."

At half past seven she threw off the covers. I wondered what would happen next, but she stayed lying there - apparently she was unable to stand the heat any longer. The total indifference with which she thrust at me her backside clothed only in lacy panties was derisive. I could actually feel myself being pushed down the social ladder.

"Fine," I said, I'll just have a shower and I'll be right with you."

It didn't sound at all the way I'd intended.

After that I thought it better to say nothing at all.

At seven fifty-four I got up without saying goodbye and went downstairs. Kral arrived almost at once - he was all red, and there was a faint smell of beer on his breath. His wife took his sweat-sodden gear from him.

"So how did it go?" he enquired jovially, but there was no fooling me this time.

"It didn't go at all."

He looked suddenly startled:

"What you mean - not at all?"

"Just that: *not at all.*"

"Did they stay home?" Kral said suspiciously. It was a question to his wife. She nodded.

"I'm packing it in," I said.

"*Packing it in?*" Kral said with scorn. "But you haven't even started..."

I did not have the strength to be drawn into any sort of discussion.

"I'm not up to it."

"Why give up right at the outset?"

"Why? Because I managed to get only one sentence out of her for the whole two hours."

My words had an unexpected effect on the couple.

"Wha-a-t?" said Kral. "She said something?"

"What did she say?" said Mrs Kralova, in the same manner in which she had earlier asked about *my* daughter. Her interest this time was far more intense, though.

"That I was going to have my work cut out - or words to that effect."

The couple exchanged glances.

"Out loud?" Kral asked.

"What?"

"Did she say it *out loud*?"

"Yes. Out loud. And all on her own."

He couldn't understand.

"Come with me," he instructed me cheerily. He steered me into his fine office and paid me ten thousand crowns *as an advance on July*.

"She'll give in, you'll see!" he assured me.

Not long ago, I came across an interview with the National Theatre actor Boris Rösner in *Lidové noviny*. In answer to the question, What did he regard as his greatest success to date, he replied: *I believe the greatest success I have had in my life so far is to have a fine, bright and healthy eighteen-year-old daughter.*

What's wrong with that?

III

1. That very evening I tried to reflect on the entire situation, but I don't recall coming to any significant conclusion.

Next morning, there was constant coming and going in our office.

The first to come in was our colleague Stribrny, an eighteen-year-old grammar school drop-out. In faltering tones he told us he was on the run from his class of fourteen-year-olds, and with the expression of a cornered roe-deer he asked us to offer him asylum until the bell. From the other side of the door could be heard the gradually fading cries of a frenzied mob.

"Stop fucking us about, Stribrny!" someone shouted to the sound of stamping feet.

See what I mean? his expression said. He looked exhausted in spite of his youth.

"You mustn't let them become too familiar," the others reproved him in friendly fashion.

He nodded sadly.

"That's what they all say - but how do you *do* it?"

There was no time for an answer as colleague Trakarova arrived in high dudgeon wanting colleague Chvatalova-Sukova *to clarify certain matters regarding tomorrow's educational concert.* But Chvatalova-Sukova was not present.

"Where is she - our *artiste*?"

"In the Principal's office."

"What is she doing with him there all the time - fornicating?" she laughed.

Svetlana Trakarova was one of very few women teachers who was truly aware how great and also how dangerous was the debt which communist education (with its hypocritical puritanism

34

known as *socialist morality*) had left behind in the field of sexual education, and she had made it her life's mission to wipe it out or at least reduce it considerably. It must be said that she was particularly well fitted for this - by no means easy - task because, unlike the dyed-in-the-wool conservatives such as Jaromir Nadany (whose reactionary attitudes were typified by his celebrated declaration that *not even the Czech Republic's possible pre-eminence in the number of infected young people would compel him to discuss with children the auto-erotic aid Greedy Mouths*) she felt no false modesty. On the contrary, the totally open approach she adopted in her family education classes towards matters that were until recently taboo was a certain source of gratification to her.

On that particular Monday morning, she was carrying under her arm a pile of some two hundred fresh photocopies of a cross-section of a vagina (although on reflection, it might have been a cross-section of a uterus) the various parts of which her pupils had to describe in tests. Tests of this type are based on the well-tried principle of unmarked geographical maps, the only difference perhaps being that instead of *Asia Minor*, you write *labia majora*.

"Would you believe that nine boys out of ten in seventh year are unable to find the clitoris?" she informed us in consternation.

"But *how*?" colleague Stribrny repeated forlornly.

Happily, the main focus of Svetlana's interest that morning was the aforementioned educational concert.

"Why do we have to go to an educational concert *four* times a month?" she fumed. "Once a year would be more than enough..."

"Because music," Jaromir declared sweetly, "is the food of love."

Sadly I was not to be allowed to hear the remainder of the conversation because shortly after Svetlana's arrival, I was summoned to the Principal's study by the school secretary - I can well imagine your eventual objections, but after all I have never maintained that *every* dialogue that you read is a legally authenticated tape recording. *The author indicates stylistically to his readers that their hero is the author himself and that the precisely described conflicts are*

his own, while at the same time unsettling us by "make believe",
fabrications and patent exaggeration, so that it is impossible to
confirm the identity without risk of error. Milan Jungmann on
Rudolf Sloboda.

Apparently the Principal was planning a fishing trip on this occasion, as he was wearing the off-duty uniform of Corporal J.Q.
Adams. (It occurs to me, after what I said above that it would be
worth stressing here that this is not a *fabricated* name.)

"Are you bringing me your notice?" he said, the moment I entered that electrical goods store which some of my colleagues (for
reasons I prefer not to examine) still called the Principal's study. It
didn't matter a jot to him that he had summoned me and should
therefore be the better informed why I was there. He used to fire
that question automatically at every teacher entering, so that it
should be understood that the possible departure of the teacher in
question would have no effect on the survival or otherwise of *his*
Vladislav Vancura school, since dozens of other (*i.e.*, better)
teachers were waiting outside the gates.

"Take a seat."

I remained standing, with the intention of getting the visit over
with as quickly as possible. Our mutual hostility had been an open
secret for a long time already so not even Corporal J.Q. Adams
found anything strange in this.

"That speech of yours about Vancura...," he said, deep in
thought. He tried to find it on his desk, but the large number of
competition entry forms, small-ad magazines and coupons for the
game *Stake a hundred - win a million!* somewhat complicated his
task.

"I think it might be under that tin of fishing spinners," I said
helpfully. And it was.

"I don't like it," he said outright.

"I'm pleased to hear it," I said. "That could mean that it's
actually good."

"It's not good!"

"Why?"

"There's too much about Vancura."

36

It was a well-known fact that the name of that leftwing intellectual in the school's title was a thorn in the Principal's flesh.

"I understand."

"You'll re-write it."

"I assume that was a question. The answer is no."

He glanced over at the boxes of televisions, videorecorders and microwave ovens stacked by the wall as if these proven commercial achievements were evidence of his qualifications in the field of literary history:

"I'll write it *myself!*"

"The National Literary Memorial will sue you," I warned him. He shrugged.

"You won't be getting a bonus or a merit rating."

"Not even if I bring you some worms?"

True to form, he ordered me out of his office.

Although, thanks to Kral, I wasn't short of money, it was a matter of principle, as usual. So that afternoon I drafted a rather emotively tinged complaint (*... in the hands of the Principal, Mr Naskocil, the apportioning of personal bonuses and premiums is increasingly becoming a tool for settling scores with his opponents...*), which I sent by registered mail to Dr Jiri Najmon, D.Ed., Director of the Education Department for Prague 5. I quote verbatim from his reply:

At meeting with Principal, Mr Naskocil, regarding your complaint, I was informed as follows. When introducing optional bonuses and personal premiums, Principal adopted criteria by which he is guided. Teaching staff were informed of them. Principal has full powers to determine and evaluate pedagogical staff. The Ed. Dept. can hardly apportion optional payments ad lib, without knowledge of work of individual teachers. According to Principal's statement, you apparently failed to fulfil established criteria.

Yours sincerely, etc.

A Successful Celebration

*The fiftieth anniversary of the tragic death of the great Czech
writer Vladislav Vancura, executed fifty years ago by the German
gestapo, has also been commemorated by the pupils of the Vladislav Vancura Elementary School at a commemorative celebration.
In his speech, the school's Principal, Mr Naskocil, emphasised the
decisive role of the Americans in the liberation of our country by
the Soviet Army and, as always, the school choir under the baton of
Mrs Chvatalova-Sukova provided the cultural program. The
warmest reception was reserved for that traditional favourite, the
'Sorrow of Love Polka' by Zbraslav-born composer Jaromir Vej-
voda, which the members of the choir sang in its world-renowned
English version, 'Roll on the Barrels'. However, the crowning
event of the successful celebration was the closing appearance by
members of the local branch of the Military Vehicle Club in which
the Principal himself took part in a U.S. Army jeep.* (Zbraslav
News, 7/1992, p.2)

I believe our education system is waking up nicely. Petr Pitha,
Minister of Education.

2. I walked home in the company of Jaromir.
   "Didn't you ever have Beata Kralova in Czech class?" I asked
him straight out. "Some six or eight years ago?"
   "I did," he said without lengthy reflection.
   "What sort of pupil was she? Anything like Agata?"
   "By no means," Jaromir said. "She was a *top student*."

We parted company at the Belvedere, and I walked onwards in
the direction of the upper school to meet my daughter. She could,
incidentally, have attended the lower school, where I was teaching,
but my wife and I wanted to spare her the awkward fate of the
teacher's child for her first four years at least. (Now - as I write
this in January 1994 - she is already in fourth year and by rights

ought to continue down there as of September, but even though I no longer teach there, she will be obliged on account of Daddy's writing, to travel all the way to Chuchle every day, poor thing.)

She saw me from a distance and started running to meet me. (Yes, I also realise that the image of *a little nine-year-old girl running to meet her adored Daddy with a satchel on her back and plaits swinging* is hardly recommendable in terms of the writer's craft, but I have to keep it in, because it sometimes occurs to me that in some strange way it has an indirect bearing on the whole story.)

"Hello," she said and kissed me.

She's not ashamed of me yet.

I removed the load of school books from her dainty shoulders: "Hello."

An ironic glint came to her brown eyes:

"I expect you want to know *how I spent the day*?"

It was obvious to me what she was getting at: as a specialist I was naturally aware that the parent's invariable question *How was it at school?* is a mistake pedagogically and psychologically speaking, since, to an inadmissible degree, it restricts life's rich diversity to schooling - but on the other hand I have never made the effort to come up with some variations on the question *How did you spend the day*, which whilst being pedagogically and psychologically sound had become rather monotonous by dint of constant repetition.

"I'm *really* interested to hear," I said with a guilty smile.

She gave me a searching look.

"What about Riha - is he still in love with you?" I said. "Or is he two-timing you with a Ninja turtle?"

She rolled her brown eyes upwards, but took me by the hand regardless. I changed my pace to suit hers.

"What about lunch?" I said. "Is it time for me to get up another petition?"

"Dill sauce," she said tersely. "It was OK."

It occurred to me that our conversation lacked a certain poetic dimension. After a while I said:

"Did it ever strike you that school holidays have their own special scent?"

She turned her head towards me suspiciously. Something in my expression apparently gave me away because she said:

"You don't have to try - anyway I know that you're really only interested in marks."

She took immediate advantage of her momentary superiority (in this she takes after her mother):

"I bought myself a *Bravo*, is that OK?"

I hesitated.

"That's OK," I said, with a certain lack of conviction. "It's *your* pocket money".

"It's got songs *in English* too," she said in a transparent attempt to prove the educational value of the incriminated magazine.

I recalled the middle-page spread *Love, sex and tenderness* that had slightly annoyed me the previous time.

"Among other things," I said scornfully.

She blushed *red as any rose.*

Stay as young as you are, I silently instructed her. I decided not to taunt her any more.

"Michael Jackson slipped from second place down to number nine," she told me hastily.

I shrank in horror:

"How can you tell it to me just like that?! My life has lost all meaning now! How about you?"

"And that's something I really can't stand...," she said. The alacrity with which she shifted from defence to attack again reminded me of her mother, "...the way you're always making fun of me..."

I'm mad about Michael Jackson and would like a black pen-friend who looks like him (though he doesn't have to). I'm twelve years old. Michaela Lipajevova, Sartoriova 29, 169 00 Prague 6. *Bravo.*

Before going off to see Beata, I sorted through my old notes and jottings and took a couple of things with me.

Neither Kral nor his wife was home. Agata made me coffee with a display of reluctance.

"What's new?" I asked.

"Irish stew!" she snapped insolently.

"And apart from that," I said, "Michael Jackson has slipped from second to ninth place!"

"So what?" said Agata and slammed the door behind her.

That's that then, I thought to myself. Now the other one.

3. She didn't react to my knock this time either.

Neither the room nor Beata's pose betrayed any visible change since the previous day; only the gloom was noticeably deeper on account of the overcast sky. I went over to the desk and mutely switched on a little halogen lamp. A swivel chair on castors stood at the desk. I pushed it over to the oil barrel onto which I tossed my file of notes. It made a slight thud, and Beata's head moved just perceptibly on the pillow. She's still alive, I thought to myself. I could see not the slightest reason to spare this spoiled primadonna in any way.

I commenced the lesson with *Advice for a Budding Writer* by Anton Chekhov:

"It is very easy to become a writer. Every cripple will find a partner and every nonsense a suitable reader," I read. *"So don't lose heart... Place a sheet of paper in front of you, pick up a pen, and having needled your inquiring mind, write rapidly. Write about anything you like: prunes, the weather, the hands of the clock, last year's snow... When you have written it, pick it up, feeling the sacred trembling in your veins, and take it to an editor. Then go home and lie down on the divan, spit at the ceiling and bask in your dreams..."*

I fell silent.

"So I assume you've already written something?" I said spitefully.

She still lay there motionless.

"Will you let me read it?"

41

Nothing.

"A pity," I said. "Proust says that one should know a writer solely through his books and not personally. *No one would find a creature less like his books, a more conceited, more affectedly august or more disagreeable companion,* he writes word for word. - I fear that that applies to us *both...*"

All of a sudden her pale, drawn face appeared alongside the barrel.

"Fuck off," she said slowly with exemplary diction.

She said nothing else for the remaining one hundred and fifteen minutes.

As for me, I just went on behind her back with my lecture as normal (if that word fits here) according to my original plan: I acquainted her with my six-year-old, but still extremely persuasive analysis of *Lady with a Little Dog*, which I went on to use as an ideal springboard for an effective, though also erudite exposure of all the key mysteries of the short story genre. Even though my voice betrayed that familiar forced dignity of the speaker who is obliged to finish his address in spite of the fact that no one is listening, my conviction never waned for one moment that, amazingly, I had her attention - it must have been the same sort of irrational conviction as when a woman in her third month talks to a patently deaf embryo while persuading herself and her husband that their little David or little Jane can *definitely hear it*.

When I was transcribing the above lines today, I once more conjured up my lonely monologue of that time and I thought of another comparison: In fact it's the same thing as *writing* - I am also sending sentences out into the void, aren't I... (Not that I'm complaining by any means; after all it's still better than having - God forbid - the face of some Polish humorist, some Jaromir Slomek, staring at you when you're writing.)

At eight o'clock precisely I put away my notes and went downstairs. Kral came out of his office. He had bags under his eyes.

"It went marvellously," I said before he had a chance to ask. "She told me to fuck off."

He laughed delightedly.

"Out loud," I added. "How much do I get?"

This time he grasped my meaning.

"I'd like to talk to you," I said.

He nodded me towards the office.

Mrs Kralova watched us go with concern in her eyes.

The cheerlessness of the two-foot-high pile of files on the oak desk was not relieved even by that splendid golden lamp. Kral went over to the bar and the familiar scent of leather armchairs mingled with the fragrance of 12-year-old Glen Deveron scotch. I had no intention of being placated, however:

"Let's summarise the situation," I said resolutely. "Since yesterday I have spent a total of four hours here."

He bided his time.

"In the course of those four hours your daughter spoke precisely twice. A total of *seven* words."

I let it resonate.

"It's all right," Kral said with a show of impatience. "It'll sort itself out."

I leaned forward:

"All right? She says seven words in four hours and it's all right? She totally ignores me. A course is quite out of the question - and it's all right? How come?"

"It'll sort itself out," he repeated reassuringly. His tanned face was wrinkled.

"Look here," I insisted, "she says *You can say that again* and in return you paid me ten thousand. What am I supposed to make of it, for heaven's sake?"

He avoided my gaze.

"So at least come up with some acceptable explanation so that I might have something to bolster my notorious tendency to self-deception," I appealed to him. "It doesn't even have to be true, for God's sake..."

He laughed.

I didn't.

"You're overdramatising it," he said. "The girl's simply got the blues. She broke off with a fellow - you know the scene... She just needs *cheering up* a bit."

That was news to me.

"Cheering up? Not *writing*, then?"

"Writing, as well, why not?" Kral said. "We'll see what helps her most. After all, you're the expert when all's said and done."

"I am? What do you take me for - a psychologist?"

At first I meant to say *psychiatrist*.

"You've studied *pedagogy*, you're a *writer*, you've got a daughter too..." he enumerated with conviction. He smiled: "You don't even know yet that you're the winner of my secret competition!"

"I am?"

"You wouldn't expect me to have got some woman teacher in, would you? - She'd have eaten her alive."

He pronounced the words *woman teacher* with undisguised dread.

Who would have eaten whom? I pondered.

"A teacher is a *profession*," he said, using the well-known joke. "A woman teacher is a *diagnosis*."

I laughed politely.

It was his turn to lean forward:

"I just don't want her to destroy herself this way. I want her to do something *sensible* - I don't care what. She can go swimming, for instance, invite her girlfriends over for a birthday party... Just so long as she doesn't meet any *looneys*."

"Looneys?"

He brushed the question aside:

"She used to go out with one once."

He had something on his mind.

"Do you understand now what I want of you?"

"Some sort of pedagogical-cum-psychological service," I said. "As performed by *the engineer of human souls*."

Fortunately he was scarcely listening to me.

"To stop her being unhappy, that's all."

44

(With the best will in the world I am incapable of describing in a convincing and unsentimental way the enormous weight of paternal love that was borne by that sentence.)

We drank in silence.

"Happiness - " I eventually said nonplussed, " - that's hardly something you can *teach*."

"Take yourself - " he said cunningly, " - you're not unhappy, are you?"

I reflected.

"Not really," I conceded.

"There you are, then!" he said triumphantly. "Just show her how you do it..."

IV

1. "And if you manage to make the sad princess laugh," my wife asked me at breakfast, "will he give you her hand in marriage, at least?"

Nonchalantly she spread cheese on her toast. I glanced at my daughter and saw she was listening intently.

"I'm married already," I said. "I'm going to ask for the *entire* kingdom."

The metro entrance hall at Smichov Station - the traditional assembly point before educational concerts - buzzed merrily. Whereas the girls paraded rather aimlessly up and down the hall, teetering on unaccustomed high heels (while swinging their cumbersome handbags), almost all of the boys present swarmed like bees around their teacher, Miss Trakarova, who stood facing the condom vending machine on the wall and with the expression of a pioneer of sexual enlightenment, eschewing any false modesty, was loudly selecting for them the most dependable types or helping them unjam a five-crown coin. With the exception of our colleague Chvatalova-Sukova, who with gesticulations of someone conducting Wagner's *Twilight of the Gods* was trying to make some point or other to the petrified stationmaster. The remaining members of the pedagogical escort team were standing in a small, embarrassed huddle, evading the glances of passers-by and trying to ignore the din made by the non-stop pillage of the vending machine. In an attempt to get away from there as soon as possible, I simply nodded to them briefly and quietly gave the order to depart:

"Let's go," I called in an undertone.

Whenever I was in public I had certain difficulties in finding my teacher's voice, because - even after several years' experience -

I could never manage to overcome my unease in the face of such phrases as *Line up, Class 8C.*

Admittedly two or three girls from my class did hear my order, but as soon as they discovered that the required stampede had not yet occurred, they looked straight through me and continued their promenade. I had to raise my voice.

"Hanka, Kamila! Come on!"

An elderly couple walking by at that very moment immediately stopped to get a look at a unique specimen of *Czech male teacher in action.* Their obvious delight was not entirely unlike the often seen elation of visitors to a zoo on coming upon the crested baboon at feeding time.

Hanka and Kamila shuffled up to become the first, distressingly isolated, pair.

"Ladya!" I called.

Ladya came and stood reluctantly behind the two girls. Our colleague Chvatalova-Sukova's annually proclaimed ban on the wearing of jeans or any denim accessories to the educational concerts had had a fairly crucial effect on his present attire: the requisite dark trousers, most likely his father's, were really too big for him, a fact that he tried to conceal by tightening the leather backwoodsman's belt as much as possible. A packet of Wild Tiger condoms showed through the breast pocket of his white nylon shirt.

"Line up, 8C!!" I bawled mightily.

In the foyer of the Municipal Library concert hall, packed with young friends of serious music from five Prague schools, the strains of *Einer Kleiner Nachtmusik* heralded the start of the program of Mozart selections with commentary. I led my class over to a relatively peaceful location in front of the men's toilets, where I made a brief appeal complete with several virile reproaches regarding the earlier problems at Smichov Station.

"Any questions?" I asked at the end, deliberately imitating the phraseology and diction of the fearsome Lt Col Brabec.

"Can I listen to my walkman?" Jana mumbled, ostentatiously gripping her nose between thumb and forefinger.

"No. Any other questions?"

"But I don't like Mozart," she protested.

"Me neither!"

"Me neither!"

Even though I knew all too well that the impending mutiny could be prevented only by nipping it in the bud, I did permit myself a moment's hesitation.   I turned towards the concert hall, which in the meantime had started to fill: Chvatalova-Sukova was leaning serenely against the rail of one of the boxes, her eyes half closed.   She was evidently awaiting the further resurrection of musical genius with intense excitement.   For a moment I forgot my pupils and mused privately on what might happen if at that moment some elegant man in a white rococo wig were to approach my colleague and whisper to her the word *Bertramka*, for instance. No doubt it was such musings as those that gradually brought on an attack of that most insidious of teachers' diseases - pedagogical nihilism.

"All right, then," I said, "which *other* Praguers do not understand the Master?"

This was too difficult.

"Who else doesn't like Mozart?" I said in their parlance.

A forest of hands.

"Fine - so you listen to what you *do* like."

They couldn't believe their ears.

"Can we have them, then - " Vlastik Lizanek asked doubtfully, " - our walkmen?"

My single populist nod made me the hero of the day.   With victorious whoops they stormed into the hall.   I strolled after them with my hands in my pockets, but at the sight of the respectable First Republic costumes of the two elderly ushers, I shrank back from my own boldness:

"But not till the lights go out!" I called after them cravenly, breaking into a trot.

Only some of the lights went out.

"By his eighteenth birthday...," explained the concert presenter, staring with a hurt expression at Vlastimil Lizanek who, with black headphones on his ears, was just pulling his neighbour's elbow towards him to assist his imitation of an electric guitar player, "...by

48

his eighteenth birthday, the young Mozart had created over *two hundred* musical compositions."

But the sudden howl from her microphone had greater effect on the audience than Mozart's commendable diligence.

"Shhh!" a number of the women teachers hissed together. They were standing along both sides of the hall, their gaze fixed chiefly on the auditorium.

"Two hundred compositions. By the age of eighteen. Just imagine it," the presenter repeated.

Here we go again: *shining examples, fitting models.*

Once more we are forcing them *to kneel at the foot of oppressive monuments* (Siegfried Lenz).

"Silence!"

The admonition on this occasion was not directed at any of my charges, but it did cause Chvatalova-Sukova to open her eyes and register for the first time not merely the scandalous fact that about one third of the pupils of Class 8C had headphones on their ears, but even worse, the inexplicable reality that their class teacher, no doubt under the influence of some drug or other, seemingly approved.

"Take those off!" she hissed, and threw an apologetic glance in the direction of the stage.

The presenter gave a slight nod.

"Mozart created clear, playful and often even humorous music," the presenter said in a clear and almost playful voice.

There followed an illustration.

"Zeleny!" Chvatalova-Sukova ejaculated *sotto voce* amidst the music. "Your last warning!"

Zeleny pulled off the headphones and theatrically removed the two batteries before stuffing them up his nostrils. He looked a bit like a character out of Star Wars, but in my mood at that moment I was ready to consider it a legitimate gesture of protest against *The Marriage of Figaro*. My colleague's dumb show, however, suggested that we tended to differ in our assessment of his action.

"Melodically speaking, it is warm, lyrical music full of unaffected joy, good humour and composure," the presenter continued meanwhile.

"Zvara!"

This time the irritated voice was Irenka's. Zvara calmed down for a moment, but the very next musical illustration had an unexpected inspirational effect on him: he unobtrusively slipped his arms round the shoulders of the girls on either side of him - seated there by Irenka at the beginning of the concert in a naïve attempt to isolate him from other problem pupils, and in a surprise attack he allowed his hands to slip the requisite few inches lower.

The girls shrieked in alarm.

"Cosy fan titties!" Zvara exclaimed with unfeigned joy.

"Zvara!" Irenka yelled and bent forward to make a dash for the perpetrator. I must admit I had a certain sympathy for Zvara as my own first touch of a girl's breasts was in the Prague Planetarium and in very similar circumstances, but as Irenka squeezed past me, I nonetheless shot her a look conveying a colleague's sincere understanding.

"Zeleny's nicked my cassette!" Kamila complained loudly.

"I didn't!" Zeleny protested. "I hid it!"

"Silence!" several of the women teachers chorused.

Remembering Beata, I found this paradoxical.

The presenter projected another slide, but my view of the composer Dussek and his wife was obscured by an inflated condom.

And so on.

I started to have my doubts.

Part of the Windows program manager that I am using to write this book is a command called *Auto-Arrange*. *(Auto-Arrange will be welcomed by all perfectionists and anyone who dislikes chaos.* Michael Hruska, Windows 3.1) - could it be that I am doing the same thing when I arrange all the chaos in my head into clear chapters?

Others also raise their doubts on occasions. When I was telling Beata's story just recently to my friend the Brno publisher Martin Pluhacek, he was less than convinced, to judge from his expression:

"That's not the problem - it's a great *story*," he reflected. "It's just that, is it feasible at all to *write* about suicide?"

I knew what he meant.

"It has to be!"

With fervour I expounded to him the *understatement* method.

2. Every pedagogue returning to our office after enduring an educational concert reminded me of a beaten prisoner being brought back to his cell after interrogation: his movements would be similarly torpid, and he too would receive immediate care and attention. We were no exception: Irenka instantly collapsed onto the chair which Jaromir had promptly pushed in her direction, and Liba obligingly put the kettle on for coffee.

"Janacek?" Lenka empathised, pouring us each out a tot of Becherovka, the national restorative.

"Mozart," I said. "And Sukova and Trakarova."

"Heavens," Jaromir said in the tones of an authority. "*A concert with commentary.* Seventy-five minutes non-stop. And lights on in the hall."

"You'd better have another one, then," said Lenka.

"And problems with the microphone," I said, "*inter alia.*"

"And with condoms," Irenka added.

She went on to explain.

"You've had a real time of it," Libuska said with feeling.

"On the other hand, though," Jaromir slowly announced with a twinkle in his eye, "you definitely didn't spend forty minutes hanging upside down from the gymnastic rings like our colleague Stribrny."

Even Irenka rallied on hearing this news:

"Wh-a-at?!"

"Ninth years," I said.

"They tied him by the laces and hauled him up to the ceiling," Libuska explained in greater detail.

"And set him swinging," said Lenka.

I looked at Jaromir in disbelief, but he nodded in agreement:

"He gave them a written test this morning," he said. "About bats."

Pranks. *Schoolboys and masters.*

"Can't you help it?" Beata used to say to me when I was *wise-cracking*, as she called it.

Once she read me a bit of Anaïs Nin: *I was ashamed of his opti-mism, of his effort to sort everything out:*

Can I help it? Besides, why is it that my every serious creative intention always degenerates into farce? Most likely out of exces-sive consideration for the reader - I call it the *hospitality syndrome.* You know, feeling a duty to look after one's guests and entertain them. *Are you sure there's no draught from that window, Mrs Curinova? Have you all got something to drink? Have you all got something to laugh at?*

Keep people cheerful. Avoid mentioning illnesses. I've carried it with me since childhood: *You have to be nice to Grandad now he's got that tumour. Try and cheer him up - how about telling him about how your scooter fell in the cesspit... You're expecting guests, and your wife stabs you in the neck with the scissors? Say you cut yourself shaving...* I'm obviously not bold enough to tell the truth and so I tell sweetening lies. I'm a shameful coward because I lack the courage to deprive several thousand tired employees of their last remaining good humour. So I play the clown and add a bit of hope like whipped cream to a cup of coffee that's too bitter: *Suicide, you say? All right, but otherwise it was fun on the whole, wasn't it?*

But I'm jumping the gun.

I took advantage of the jocular mood that reigned in our office following the news about colleague Stribrny's misfortune to inform my colleagues incidentally, as it were, about my *sideline*; there was no postponing it any longer. In an effort to make the news as in-nocuous as possible I presented my new job as standard coaching, but even so my objective was thwarted.

"Kral?" Irenka exclaimed with unfeigned horror. "That *ma-fioso*? That *pimp*?"

"Frailty," said Jaromir sweetly, "thy name is woman."

"Well, am I wrong?" Irenka parried.

"Mafioso?" I said. "How can you tell?"

"Easily. When someone owns - here in Zbraslav alone - two wine bars, two hotels and a brothel in Zabehlice, it's not difficult at all. What sort of money do you think is involved in those?"

True to tradition she had an admirable grasp of what makes Zbraslav tick.

(At this point I remind the reader of my pact with Kral and stress that the list of properties mentioned is entirely and deliberately distorted.)

"There's a brothel here?" Libuska exclaimed with genuine surprise. "Where?"

"In Zabehlice," said Lenka.

Irenka did not smile.

"Irenka," Jaromir said, "could you recognise dirty money if you saw it? Not even the Prime Minister could..."

"I could," said Irenka with conviction. "I've got a nose for it."

With that she started to leave for lunch.

"I'd just be worried," she said, turning to me as she went out the door, "that you'll burn your fingers with that commie creep..."

I had no time for any deeper consideration of her words, as Lenka and Jaromir immediately started to regale me with reminiscences about that *model pupil* Beata Kralova: there was no comparing her with her younger sister, they said. Jaromir actually managed to dig out a photo from the 1983-84 school year - when she would have been eleven or thereabouts. She was sitting in the first row in a white lace blouse, her hands - as per the photographer's instructions - clasped in the lap of her blue denim skirt (it was that well-known, aggressive denim blue you find on coloured photos from poor-quality film). Her legs were tanned, and she wore white socks and worn slippers. I had a vague, fleeting feeling of tenderness mingled with amusement.

"A real doll," said Jaromir.

"There really is a brothel in Zabehlice?" I asked, since I lived nearby.

"Search me," he said. "But it ain't no ice cream parlour, that's for sure."

I went off to the school dining hall in search of Irenka. On the asphalt playground in front of the school the ninth years were running sixty-metre races - Doubek in particular drew my attention. Colleague Andelova stood at the finishing line, a stopwatch in her outstretched arm.

"Hi, Helena."

"Hi," she said wearily. Her two forearms were swathed in about a dozen wrist watches, and each time she raised her arm she looked like a mournful traffic cop. Doubek at last sprinted to the line and wheezed off to sprawl on the warm steps with the other boys. I went over to them; they were sweaty and dusty and many of them - in spite of endless university theses analysing the question of suitable P.E. gear for students - had wrinkled penises peeping out of their red shorts. They gazed at me suspiciously.

"How! I come in peace," I said, "to pow-wow with Doubek my brother redskin."

I glanced in the direction of his crotch:

"And his red foreskin."

I read into their laughter a hopeful indication that I might not be obliged to spend several school hours suspended from the gymnasium ceiling.

"What gives?" Doubek said, after adjusting his dress.

"Your farewell speech," I reminded him. "There's not much time left."

"Yeah - oh yeah," he remembered. "I'm about to write it..."

"*About to?* You said you'd already written it."

"Well, I have, more or less," he reassured me. "No sweat - I'll finish it."

"Please do," I said. "Please *finish* it."

Irena was already on her way out, so there was nothing for it but to join Steve at the table. It looked like it was going to be a really tough day.

Steve taught English, because during the 1991-92 school year they hadn't yet started to jail American language assistants for teaching English. I rather liked him (*I like Americans for their healthiness and optimism.* Franz Kafka), but I found in his presence that my language hang-ups were always heightened, not to mention the fact that at the sight of his gleaming white teeth I unaccountably found myself running my tongue over my amalgam fillings. For the reasons stated I tended to avoid him, but now there was no escape.

"Hi, Steve. How are you?" I said in my Zbraslav English.

He told me he was fine. Then he said something about some concert or other, about a delayed flight and about suntan lotions. I said that powerful suntan lotions were now a must *unfortunately,* on account of the hole in the sky. He gave me a searching look and said something along the lines of: girls should never surprise us - if I knew what he meant. I said I was well aware of the fact and added that *every cloud has a silver lining* (which was one of the three English sayings I could remember). He concurred, albeit rather uncertainly. I swallowed two dumplings at once and pointed out that it was rather hot today *unfortunately*. He was surprised to find me in such a hurry. I said that I was *unfortunately* very busy.

I have never eaten my lunch so fast in my life.

Believe me, that American is not here just for decorative purposes.

In other words: *The meaning of art is not in the punch line.* Jan Zabrana.

Another NB: Last year in Hamburg, I asked Karel Trinkewitz, among other things, what he thought about the use of quotations in contemporary writing. He subsequently sent me his essay "On the Post-Modern Novel", in which he had underlined the following quotation from Roland Barthes: *No originality ever exists. We inhabit a certain kind of great exchange, a great intertext. Ideas circulate; language likewise. Meanwhile, the only thing we can do, and get into the habit of, is combining them. But there is one idea not yet created after all: it is here, like a sort of major market in a major economy. Thoughts circulate and only at a certain moment are stopped and sorted out, and are then edited, probably as when making a film, and that produces a work.*

Well, there you are.

3. On my return home I put back again the notes about writing, and for a change I tried to dig out some ideas on the subject of human happiness. *Happiness is the art of being satisfied.* Bergmann.

And others.

I literally dragged myself to the Krals', as the heat was truly unbearable.

Agata was still not speaking to me.

Her parents weren't home.

In the attic room just one discernible change had occurred: there was a smell of wine. I focused my eyes in the gloom: a bottle stood on the bedside table. Beata was covered merely with a crumpled sheet - I was not entirely certain, but she struck me as being naked. A duvet was lying on the floor by the bed. Both facts perturbed me somewhat, so I preferred not to switch on the light and moved the typist's chair I was sitting on nearer to the bookcase, as if the spines of the books which I now touched with my fingertips - most of them familiar titles - could somehow safely earth the tension I felt. I pondered at length on how I might even start until, for want of a better idea, I ended up using Kral's thought from the day before: Am I unhappy? No, I'm not, broadly speaking. So I'll simply show her how I manage it:

I strive to *search for good omens* (Doctorow).

I strive to *love life more than its meaning* (Dostoevsky).

I strive to *scour my past years for the sediment of habits and passions that I may consider typical and enduring for me, and those I cherish above all so that life, as I have chosen it, should bring me happiness* (Proust).

I strive not to lose my sense of humour, because *only a joke can reconcile us with the farce of life* (S.J. Lec) and because *so long as you're laughing you're always safe* (K. Kesey).

I strive to observe certain rules, because *rules are all we have* (Golding).

I strive to *endorse every interpretation of the universe that is conducive to kindness* (Simecka), and do not strive to read and understand everything, because *a lack of education can also be a source of strength and peace of mind* (Italo Svevo), particularly since *all I really need to know I learned in kindergarten* (Fulghum).

I strive to like myself and try every time to forget as quickly as possible what party certain of my friends voted for.

I strive not to buy lottery tickets and not to bet on the Sure-Win.

I strive to drink just enough to relax without wrecking myself.

I strive to avoid dances and department stores.

I strive to keep my eyes to myself in the men's sauna.

In the dentist's waiting room I prefer to tell silly jokes rather than talk about gum incisions.

I do likewise in life.

Finally - now I was in my stride - I divulged to her the subtlest trick for grabbing a little bit of that happiness: *Self-sacrifice, self-limitation. If you can't save yourself, try to save your neighbour.*

The closing number of the wiliest of egoists.

It took me less than forty minutes, with the help of two dozen quotations, to solve it all: the collapse of traditional values, increasing alienation, the cult of consumerism, the crisis of the family, the loss of God and the loss of identity - and I still had ten minutes left to summarise and recapitulate. It was a *model* lesson.

I was chuffed with myself.

"Amen," Beata said.

By now she was well and truly sozzled, and I had merely *bored her by repeating sensible things* (Saul Bellow).

There was no sense in continuing. Each time she reached for the wine, the sheet would fall from her. Eventually she didn't even bother to cover herself up again. This was not for reasons of seduction, of course, but (like her greasy, unkempt hair) a matter of demonstrative, studied indifference. All the positions she adopted on the bed were purely and simply *functional* - to ease the pressure on the arm she had been lying on, in order to lean against the wall, in order to reach the wine - and the fact that in so doing she revealed to me *everything* indicated solely her total disregard for my unwanted presence.

There was a moment when she broke wind audibly without considering me worthy of even an apologetic smile.

My nose filled with humiliation.

I was unable to resist it:

"The scent of woman," I said with unconcealed distaste.

That literally incensed her.

"Piss off, then! Do you hear? Piss off! Nobody asked you to be here!"

In spite of her frenzied outburst, part of my mind remained surprisingly clear. Wow, what a profusion of words all of a sudden, I said to myself almost with gratification. Kral will have to shell out for that.

"Do you think I could give a damn about your educational drivel?" she yelled. "It won't bring him back to me!"

Who? The looney?

She collapsed onto the bed in a fit of weeping.

There, there, what a lot of tears!

She sobbed for a few moments more and then fell asleep. Red scales of wine remained on her chapped lips.

It was out of the ordinary to say the very least.

Even in the course of my own fairly nondescript sex life I had, admittedly, like everyone else, occasionally experienced a girl leaning back on her elbows on a bed and pointing her nipples at me - but none of them had ever looked at me with hostility at the same time. Their expressions had been amiable, or coquettish, or normal, or (on two regrettable occasions) amused, but never *hostile.* That unprecedented coupling of nakedness and hostility occupied my thoughts for a good few minutes.

She moaned softly.

I looked at her in surprise and noticed that she was caressing herself as she dozed.

Her liquid mother-of-pearl glittered on the rumpled sheet.

58

My concern with the philosophical aspects of her combined beauty and hostility waned somewhat.

Her mouth was dry. She struggled for breath and woke up. This time she registered my presence with mixed feelings; her face betrayed both disappointment and joy - the same sort of expression, I expect, as someone at home who suddenly gets an overwhelming craving for an ice cream sundae with fruit and whipped cream and then finds to their surprise a re-frozen, half thawed choc ice in the freezer.

"Come on," she said.

In an undertone. You get the picture.

She was already making room for me next to her.

"No way," I said.

For the life of me I couldn't come up with a suitable quotation.

"Come on!" she again commanded me.

"Oh no, Princess," I said, "I won't tie your shoe, I'm afraid."

Kral only came home to change. His driver didn't even switch off the motor.

"I need to speak to you."

"*Again*, so soon?"

He sounded dissatisfied. Couldn't I sort it out myself? Did I have to keep on bothering him with problems?

"I'm in a terrible hurry," he said curtly.

"Spare me three minutes."

"No can do."

"Two minutes!"

"Tomorrow," he said in the doorway. "I might even spare you an hour tomorrow."

I said goodnight to Mrs Kralova and set off home. In the garden I came upon Petrik and Jirik. Each of them was making a fairly good job of smashing so-called flue bricks with the edge of his hand.

"Was he working for *them*?" I eventually asked, for want of anything better to say.

They enjoyed this immensely.

"No," Jiri laughed, "he was a dissident!"

To tell the truth, it wasn't particularly bothering me at that moment.

Rather, I had a need to confide in someone. In a veiled fashion I outlined my recent problems with Beata.

"If she don't want to talk, why should she?" said Petrik. "If she wants a screw, then screw her! Where's the problem?"

"That's rich coming from you," I pointed out. "You're supposed to be protecting her."

He gave me a friendly slap in the groin. It made my eyes water - but they were waiting for the repartee.

"Yeah, I know, from weapons of a different kind; this sort isn't in your job description..."

The humorist's burden.

4. I arrived home. I assume that I greeted the dog and kissed my daughter goodnight (she would have been on her way to bed at the time I got back from the Krals', so I expect I did). I then most probably made a cup of tea with my wife and looked through various holiday brochures - thanks to Kral's money we were trying at that particular time to decide where we'd spend our vacation. So far I am only guessing - but there is one thing I have a very precise recollection of: that I was intending, if possible, to spend a peaceful evening with the family, and it is quite conceivable that I would have succeeded had my over-stimulated memory not bombarded me constantly with extremely realistic pictures of girls caressing themselves.

On the stroke of midnight someone gave a short ring on the doorbell.

My wife was already asleep. I surveyed the street from behind the curtain: Kral's highly polished car was standing right beneath our window. Petrik was standing by the doorbell; I gestured to him to come upstairs.

The moment he stepped inside I pushed him face first against the wall and, without a word, symbolically searched him (for a moment I wrestled with the thought of actually removing his pistol, but I was scared to handle it in any way).

"Get dressed," he laughed discreetly. "You're coming with us."

"Where to?"

He adopted a secretive expression.

"You got no warrant," I said.

But I was already getting dressed. I hadn't the foggiest notion where I was going or why, but I was absolutely sure that I wanted to go.

My life as a schoolmaster, until recently so sedate, was becoming an adventure.

"Am I going to read her a bedtime story?"

Petrik just smiled:

"Not your jeans," he said. "You gotta get dolled up."

I pulled the door to as quietly as possible.

The night was warm. Kral came round the car.

"I owe you that chat," he said.

I looked at my watch:

"It wasn't as urgent as that though..."

He raised his eyebrows ironically:

"So you don't want to reveal your *terrible secret* any more?"

The limousine cruised the darkened streets almost noiselessly. The trees in the surrounding gardens were caught in the headlights. Beyond the bend appeared the pitch-black bulk of the Vltava valley. I stuck my hand out of the window and placed it on the roof: the metal was cool, but not unpleasantly so.

"Midsummer Night," I remarked. "You've staged it well."

"Today?" Kral said in unfeigned surprise - I'd almost say he didn't know.

Petrik put the car into neutral: we were coasting down to the square. I leaned back on the soft headrest. Kral pulled out of his pocket a gilt hipflask, took a swig and passed it to me. I had a drink - it was his favourite scotch - and handed back the flask.

"Young girls jump across bonfires," I declared. "Treasure caves reveal themselves, and golden fern blooms in the dark woods."

"Old wives' tales," Petrik said sceptically.

I was expecting him to turn left in the direction of Prague, but instead he turned back towards Zbraslav.

We were driving to Zabehlice.

"I could do with another drink," I said.

They laughed.

The Hotel Vltava looked fairly deserted from the road, but to my astonishment the carpark in front of the entrance was almost full - cars with German license plates predominated. Above the double entrance doors, precisely in the spot where, on my good old hardworking parents' cottage there hangs a rusty horseshoe, an eye-catching red lamp hung.

Kral rang the doorbell and announced himself through the entryphone.

Someone inside immediately unlocked the door.

I was trapped.

The attendants greeted Kral in a friendly fashion. Petrik left us to go and chat with some liveried bouncer.

"Don't be crazy," I told Kral in shock, "I'm a writer with a humanist outlook. I should pillory houses of pleasure, not patronise them."

He paid not the slightest attention to me because as we walked in, he started to give the elderly man in charge of the cloakroom a ticking off for something or other, and I was obliged to follow him willy nilly. Meanwhile I tried in vain to figure out whether the underpants I was wearing didn't belong to the dreadful pink series which my wife had created during the last wash.

In contrast with the brightly lit vestibule, the lighting in the lounge was discreetly low. I noted a small but *live* band, tables with little pink lamps - scarcely half of the tables were occupied - and a single couple on the illuminated glass dance floor. The *girls* were surprisingly young and looked far better than I'd expected.

Kral turned his attention once more to me. We sat down at the bar, the high bar-stools providing a good vantage for any *action*.

"What would you like, gentlemen?" the barman asked politely.

Kral silently motioned to me to order first.

"Fried cheese," I said. "And a double portion of chips."

The barman looked at Kral.

"The gentleman is a humorist," said Kral.

He ordered champagne.

"I'm teaching first period tomorrow," I pointed out to him. "7B. I can't stay here too long."

"No problem."

He looked at one of the girls.

"It'll be a *quickie*, don't worry...," he quipped.

I gave a virile laugh, but my boyish heart began to race like a startled bird at such candour.

"Where are the bedrooms?" I inquired. My original thought was that in the given context my question would sound resolute, nay worldly, but Kral's expression gave me to understand that my inquiry was simply rather silly.

"Where do you think?" He gestured towards the broad staircase which one of the couples was just descending. "Upstairs."

Only now did the horror of the entire situation come home to me. At the same time I noticed that the woman on the dance floor was about thirty years older than her good-looking young partner.

Kral raised his glass with a smile - I was to drink a toast with him *to the success of the course.*

He scrutinised me.

"What's up?" he said shortly.

"What do you think? Nothing at all really," I said. "Just a Zbraslav schoolmaster sitting on a bar-stool at midnight in a local brothel. Quite normal."

Trakarova would give me full marks, I thought to myself.

"You take your job too seriously."

I shrugged in disagreement.

"Schoolmasters don't have sex?" Kral queried.

It niggled me, the way he abdicated any responsibility for having dragged me here.

"That's not the right question," I said. "It evades the real issue."

"So what is the right question?" he asked with a hint of pique.

There was no point in arguing with him.

"The right one? How about: *what political party does the Minister of Education belong to?*" I said. "It might not be exactly the right one, but it's certainly more specific."

The tension evaporated. But the patient, matter-of-fact way in which the redhead at the opposite table pulled one of her breasts out of her decolletage for her German partner once more threw me into consternation.

We sat drinking in silence for a while.

The young beau on the dance floor did not stop smiling for an instant.

"It's not just being in the *teaching profession*," I said after a while. "I just don't belong here *at all*. I'm a polite, well-brought-up young lad. I don't pick things up off the ground because they're *dirty*. I don't put my knife in my mouth. When my wife forgets to drain the dirty dishwater, we toss a coin to see who'll have to reach into the cold, greasy filth."

The girl had tucked in her breast. The German was sleeping with his head on the table top. The waiter once more emptied the redhead's ashtray.

"Brothels are *dirthy* too," I said. By now my articulation was not entirely without fault (whenever I get drunk an involuntary prothetic *h* slips into my speech).

"I expect I'm the proverbial timid sailor who queues for a long time and then doesn't go in," I conjectured out loud.

"It's OK," said Kral. "Don't force yourself."

I realised his tone was increasingly familiar, and he told me to call him *Denis*.

"OK, Denis."

The champagne was superb. The incongruous couple was once more circling the dance floor.

"Denis," I said cautiously, "is she sulking like that on account of the *looney*?"

"Not at all." He shook his head. "That's over and done with."

I waited, but he added nothing more.

"So what's the secret?" I asked him straight out. I actually said *thecret*, but he understood me anyway.

"There's no great secret. You'll be disappointed if I tell you."

64

His articulation was much better than mine.

"I w-h-on't."

"What's there to tell? A straightforward, unhappy love affair. What always happens when a girl falls for some rotter. A regular shyster."

My gaze was intended to convey *the fellow feeling of a father who knows what it is to have a daughter*, but I discovered from one of the many mirrors around the bar that it unfortunately conveyed nothing but intoxication.

"A shyster who made out he loved her but in fact was only after money."

He was apparently recalling an old grudge, because he raised his voice.

"So we gave him a chance - to earn some! To repay all the *harm* he'd done!"

It sounded oddly ruthless.

It suddenly struck me that his words were addressed to someone in the room. I turned to follow the line of his gaze: his eyes were fixed on the dance floor.

Kral noticed me.

"Yeah," he said sourly. "That handsome gigolo over there. He told me he was a *gardener*."

V

1. *The everlasting charm of the story.* Walter Kerr

It is unlikely to come as any surprise that my recollections of the rest of that night are confused and fragmentary. The only thing I know for sure is that after several glasses of champagne and a little cognac, the *sower's urge* (though *animal instinct* might be more accurate) can awaken in even a very well-bred lad who, on principle, does not stick his knife in his mouth or pick things up off the ground, and my ever more frequent and ever less furtive glances in the direction of the redhead with the retractable breasts were the product of lamentably primitive *lust*. After the German's departure I eventually joined her at her table - to Kral's delight - so I can truthfully boast that all the cigarettes she smoked after about two in the morning were lit by me. It was anyway the least I could do for her, since I was firmly resolved in the name of love to pick up absolutely anything from the ground or even stick it in my mouth - had she asked me to. However, she only asked me to tell her *something nice* about school, which was not particularly easy, but I think I more or less coped. It was just beginning to look as if she would reward my narrative efforts and my gallant match-wielding with that beautiful spherical prize from her de-colletage when we were unfortunately joined by the absolutely plastered Kral who, in the drunkard's customary maudlin fashion, implored me to *cure his little daughter*.

Petrik must have remained sober enough to drive us both home - although I only infer this from what I was told by my wife who, shortly after half past five in the morning caught sight of me from the bedroom window getting out of Kral's car with great difficulty.

Apparently when she asked me where I had spent the night, I answered *in a bhrothel.*

(Today, while proofreading the novel *Cape of No Hope* by Lubomir Martinek, I copied out a sentence that could well serve as a rather unpleasant indictment of myself: *The sort of humour whereby one disparages oneself in order to be assured of the contrary.*)

When the young grammar school teacher in Chekhov's short story "The Man in the Case" comes to school on a bicycle one day, his older colleague Byelikov is outraged: *When the teacher rides on a velocipede what can one expect of the pupils? They'll be walking on their heads next!*

I really have no intention of pretending that the story in question came to mind on that fateful morning when I painfully cycled the mile from the housing estate down to the school on my daughter's bike (as the chance of ridicule was far more acceptable than the risk my upset stomach would run in a stuffy bus full of children, parents and colleagues); indeed, if my throbbing head was capable of thinking at all that morning, it was certainly not about books from long ago. I half-heartedly hoped that a ride through the fresh, early morning air would help clear my head a bit, but the look of sympathy that I received from the school caretaker, Frantisek Nedelnicek, as I handed the bike over to him in front of the school, made me suspect that my hopes were more or less groundless (incidentally, however much Frantisek and I differ in our assessments of the school's most recent principals, I do quite like him, and above all I sincerely admire the almost renaissance breadth of his duties and interests which normally start on Monday morning with the firing of the school boiler, and then range through the week from amateur dramatics, puppeteering for children and competitive bowling to working on the local newspaper, and culminate on Sunday with readings of his own handwritten orations during ash-scattering ceremonies in the Garden of Remembrance at the local crematorium).

As luck would have it, there was no one but Jaromir in our office yet, and unlike Byelikov, he tended to be indulgent towards his younger colleagues.

"I'm hung over," I admitted with bald frankness, albeit rather superfluously. "What are we going to do?"

I had originally been intending to speak solely in terms of *the after-effects of a drinking bout*, but I found myself in a situation in which nausea can be brought on even by certain groupings of consonants, so I contented myself with the above-quoted simpler version. (For the benefit of teetotal readers and those exemplary individuals who always know when they have had enough, I am listing several other symptoms of that state, without which it will be impossible to share properly in the events of this chapter - they are: red, puffy, smarting eyes, alternating hot and cold flushes, quaking at the knees and a general feeling of enfeeblement, a fetid and viscous coating on the tongue, an urge to vomit, and last but not least, feelings of guilt and an irresistible urge to make resolutions.)

Jaromir brought me a chair. I needed it.

"I'll run and fetch Netejkal," he said obligingly. "He'll have some Samaritan."

A moment later Netejkal arrived in person and did nothing to conceal his satisfaction that, as he put it, *the healthy core of the school* had gained a new member as of that morning.

"Vladya," I implored him, "save me."

To crown it all, I began to feel that a hornet had stung me in the tongue on my way to school.

"I'll never touch another drop," I declared laboriously.

"Don't blaspheme," Vladimir said.

He gently bent my head backwards and put a drop of something in each of my eyes. It stung.

"It gets better," Jaromir said.

"The artist *has* to drink," Vladimir commented, "because he sees more deeply than other people."

"At this moment I can't see a thing!"

"The artist sees too much."

For some unknown reason, Vladimir obviously regarded himself as an artist.

"Because he sees double," Jaromir said.

There were only twenty minutes left to the bell.

"The first essential is to keep moving," Vladimir proclaimed, mixing some white powder in a glass of water. "Keep walking. Walk between the desks. The second one is, have the windows open. Thirdly: don't talk if you can possibly help it - too much oxygen is fatal."

His eyes glazed over momentarily as he recalled something unpleasant from the past.

"Drink this," he ordered me.

"Will he hold it down?" asked Jaromir with concern.

"Bound to," Vladimir said authoritatively. "Don't sniff it."

I closed my eyes and tossed back the contents of the glass.

I realised I had five seconds, six at the most, but certainly no more.

I leapt up out of the chair, reached the open window in two strides and threw up.

Sudden silence descended on our office. I wiped my mouth.

Vladimir cleared his throat.

"Splendid," he said. "You're out of the woods."

His optimism struck me as rather forced.

"I'll go and clear it up," I said meekly.

"Don't be daft. You don't know anything about anything - just keep your head down."

Ten minutes later - by which time our office was full - the unmistakable voice of Radek Zeleny could be heard squawking beneath the windows:

"Sir, Sir!"

Jaromir leaned out with surprising alacrity:

"Stop your yelling and get to your classroom quick-sharp!" he shouted with unaccustomed vehemence.

I was profoundly grateful.

"But Sir - "

"Didn't you hear me!" Jaromir roared mightily.

Zeleny was shocked into silence.

Jaromir stepped away from the window and sat down indignantly.

I threw him a grateful look.

"Someone has puked under your window!" Zeleny shrieked resentfully from outside.

Despite the Samaritan's failure, all my subsequent periods were hampered by my rather anxious efforts to observe Vladimir's instructions to the letter.

"It's *lovely* outside," I would say on entering the classroom. "Open the windows!"

They would look nonplussed at the overcast sky.

"Large sheets of paper. Name at the top," I would instruct them as tersely as I could, walking among the desks.

Their bewilderment would increase still further: *What? A written test right at the end of the school year? After the marks are all in?*

"This is for next year," I would silence their protests curtly.

They could not understand where my friendliness had disappeared to all of a sudden.

"It's a Ministry check-up," I invented in the case of the eighth-year class.

All my laconic remarks were directed at the ceiling.

During my fourth period, I started having hallucinations.

I was taking a class in the music room and while walking between the rows of desks, I happened to raise my eyes to the back wall, where in place of the expected maxim MUSIC IS THE FOOD OF LOVE, there was a rather different statement:

MAC IS LOVE OF FOOD.

The A in the middle looked rather unprofessional.

I wonder what was in those eye drops? I thought to myself.

"You weren't imagining things," Jaromir told me during break. "It's Kralova's prank."

2. I gave lunch a miss. I dragged myself along to the upper school where I waited for my daughter. In the course of our jolly conversation she rightly taxed me with not paying attention to her: all I could think about was going straight to bed when I got home.

I had already pulled the curtains and was just easing myself out of my clothes when the sound of Michael Jackson boomed out from her room. My hackles rose, but on the other hand I didn't want to be the father who is always saying no, not even under the present circumstances. So I went out into the passage and switched off the electricity at the mains: the silence that ensued was one of those justly called *golden*. I hastily returned to my room.

"There's another one of those power cuts," my daughter came to tell me in high dudgeon.

"It's scandalous."

She decided to go outside.

"Off you go," I said. "It's lovely out."

(I am providing this pedagogical know-how entirely free, although I should point out straightaway that over-use of this simple trick generally leads to detection, besides which, the meat in the fridge goes off.)

She came back almost immediately and was on the verge of tears.

"What happened?"

"You won't be cross with me?"

"I *hope* not."

"You *will* be cross with me."

"I won't."

"You *really* won't be cross?"

"*Really*!" I roared.

At last she plucked up courage. She gulped in woe.

"My bike's been stolen..."

I shut my eyes. Paternal shame.

"No, it hasn't," I reassured her.

I went and gargled so that I could give her a kiss.

I was still sleeping when my wife came home from work.

She pulled back the curtains and made a show of airing the room. She wore a sarcastic smile but kept close watch on me to see how guilty I was feeling, knowing as she did that in view of my poor skill at lying this was an effective way of gauging the extent

71

and seriousness of my possible sins. Among other things it also meant that she was only just making up her mind whether or not to be angry with me.

I pulled myself together in order to relate to her the story of the previous night, naturally employing a certain ironical and self-disparaging hyperbole, as well as various other well-known narrative techniques, but essentially my report was entirely truthful (I didn't even conceal my lecherous designs on the busty redhead), but she listened to me with an exceedingly sceptical expression. That got my goat: I wanted to *earn* her forgiveness fair and square by entertaining her - and she acted as if I was providing all those humorous details solely to distract her attention and make my story sound credible.

Well sod you, then, I said to myself in a huff.

I gained Agata's forgiveness rather more easily: for a tub of banana ice cream bought at the candy store in the Zbraslavanka shopping centre that I had popped into to buy some *refreshing* Orbit chewing gum while on my way to the Krals'.

"I don't want it," she said defiantly at first, of course.

She was sitting on the edge of the swimming pool, dangling her legs in the bluish water. When I sat down by her, she moved away.

"Agata," I said sincerely, "I'm sorry I shouted at you a bit the day before yesterday. I apologise."

"No one asked you to."

It was meant to sound rude, but her chin quivered as she said it.

"My nerves got the better of me," I said. "On account of your sister," I added hypocritically.

"I hate it when they yell at me..."

"Who yells at you - apart from me?"

"They all do!"

"I apologised, though."

"Yeah, you did," she acknowledged.

She was thawing like that ice cream.

"I'd like to suggest something: How about using my first name - here at home at least?"

She generously assented.

"Friends?" I asked.

"OK, then," she said.

The turning point. I realised that now - in order to set the seal on our friendship - I ought to shove her playfully into the pool, but I was in no state to deal with any *seal-splashing or other frolics* that would inevitably arise from it. I watched her licking her ice cream.

It took her aback.

"What are you staring at?"

"At your *love of food*."

She laughed:

"Good, eh?"

"Good," I praised her as she merited. "As a language teacher I liked it: it was a witty transposition."

On discovering that I was not joking, she blushed at the compliment.

"The only problem is what the teachers of the *other* subjects will say."

"What d'you think," said Agata. "They'll yell."

She wasn't far wrong.

Yesterday, under the influence of an older article by Premysl Rut, "Egoism as an Artistic Trend", I once more took stock of the embarrassing fact that I have arbitrarily appointed myself the protagonist of this book. I actually had a go at relating it in the third person:

Guy returned from the educational concert on the verge of exhaustion.

"Thank you for the coffee, Mrs Kralova," Guy said politely.

Guy learnt about Beata's suicide the night of his return from Denmark, I typed tentatively.

Then I read it back to myself.

It was immediately obvious to me that it wouldn't work.

What kind of idiot is this Guy?

Who does he think he is?

73

3. The curtains were still drawn. Beata was sitting that day in the dentist's chair. She was wearing a crumpled, shapeless T-shirt, and as I entered the room, I caught her closing her eyes apathetically.

I pulled over a chair and sat down facing her, wondering how to comfort a girl's heart, broken by the knowledge that her beloved was only a wolf in gardener's clothing. But I could only come up with hypocritical banalities or such folk sayings as *There are as good fish in the sea as ever came out of it.* I wanted at least *to show her my kindness, drawn from books* (Sandor Brody), but as ill luck would have it, I couldn't think of a single serviceable quotation.

To my surprise it was she who broke the silence half an hour later.

"Yesterday - " she said abruptly, " - was he there?"

I scarcely hesitated before deciding to give the truth a try once more that day:

"Yes."

"Did he talk to Dad?"

"Not so far as I know."

"He didn't say hello, even?"

"Oh, he said hello."

"Did Dad reply?"

"I didn't hear him reply."

Blunt, terse questions that had a harsh feel. She treated me as if I were a clerk in an information bureau in some boring provincial town. She even managed not to cast a single glance in my direction.

"How did he look?"

I hesitated.

"Very well, most people would say."

"What was he wearing?"

"A light-coloured suit with a black silk shirt."

It took her a moment to build up her courage for the final question:

"Was he... alone?"

"No."

She gnawed her lower lip like a heroine in a hot paperback romance.

She turned her face to the wall.

"Beata," I said softly, "we both know this will get you nowhere."

There are other fish in the sea.

At that moment she spun round:

"No one was asking your opinion!"

"Fine. I'll say nothing more. If you don't mind I'll have a little doze - I didn't get too much sleep last night. Should you want to know whether his partner yesterday had varicose veins, just nudge me gently."

"Kindly stop your furtive lecturing. Just stop bloody well trying to educate me!"

It was impressive, the speed at which she was working herself up:

"I'll tell you something: I can't stand teachers, and most of all I can't stand young teachers full of the joys of spring!"

She said it right into my face.

"Listen carefully: I couldn't give a damn about all the clever things you've read, I couldn't give a damn how fantastically well you hit it off with the kids, and I couldn't give a damn about your marvellous untraditional *methods*! I've no fucking interest in your marvellous *voice work*! Savvy?"

She stung me.

She stung me so much I said nothing up to seven o'clock. Some time afterwards I fell asleep.

When I came to, Beata was no longer in the room. In panic, I rushed downstairs. Petrik was sitting on the terrace.

"Look," he said, pointing into the garden full of evening shadows.

Beata was lying on her belly with her arms and legs wide outstretched.

He tapped his forehead:

"What do you reckon?"

I took another look at the face buried in the sombre lawn.

"There are two possibilities," I said. "Either she's hit rock bottom or she's spying on a mole."

...my old man blew out the chimney. Arnost Lustig
Understatement. Matter of fact.

Happily she soon returned to her room.

I remained downstairs and waited with Petrik for Kral. After a thirty-minute discourse on Ivan Lendl, the M6 automatic rifle and the film *Murderous Trap*, I readily agreed to his suggestion to go and play a game of rummy in the kitchen.

Petrik won most of the time. Mrs Kralova made us a few potato pancakes to go with our beer.

"You don't much strike me as being *on alert*," I commented.

"That's only your impression," he reassured me. "And Jirka's at the gate."

Kral arrived at nine.

"How did it go?" he asked me immediately.

He took a potato pancake. His wife wiped the oil from his chin with a napkin to stop it dripping on his shirt or tie.

"I have a favour to ask of you, Denis," I said advisedly without raising my eyes from the cards. "Could you please stop asking me how it went. As soon as it starts to go anywhere, I'll be sure to let you know. For the time being it's not working."

"Did something happen?" he said with concern.

"She can't stand me," I briefly informed him. I imitated Beata's intonation: *She can't stand teachers...*"

He laughed the contented laugh of a father whose child has perpetrated an entirely charming little prank:

"That's all right - I didn't like them either. Never did."

"Me neither," said Petrik.

"Maybe you ought to overcome your aversion for an hour tomorrow," I said. "It's the parents' conferences at school."

He said nothing, but the corners of his mouth displayed contempt.

I shrugged and turned my attention to the game.

It niggled him:

"Has Agata been up to something?"

"An innocent lark or gross vandalism, depending on the interpretation."

I briefly outlined the problem to him.

"Go and see the Principal," I advised him. "In case Chvatalova decides to make a thing of it."

"Is he someone you can talk to?" he said doubtfully.

"Not in the least," I said. "Buy him a landing net."

4. Next morning I was surprised to find on my desk about a hundred and twenty essays from the previous day. The prospect of spending several hours going through that pile on the off-chance of discovering two or three tiny nuggets of pure intelligence was daunting to say the least, but the first suckers-up were already skulking outside the office door with their intrusive questions like *How did we do?*

"You didn't do at all well," I said stony-faced. "To be quite frank most of you will be getting off to an unexpectedly poor start in the new year."

Incredulous smiles played on their lips.

"And let's be clear," I said, "I'm not joking."

They withdrew like whipped curs.

Thanks to these early morning artillery preparations for a pedagogical attack, the news of the *dreadful* results in yesterday's tests quickly spread, so that when in the different classes *out of the kindness of my heart* I subsequently tore the uncorrected tests up into bits of confetti, I garnered nothing but gratitude.

The Czech schoolmaster is not a dead myth. Petr Pitha

Standing in for a Czech literature class with 7D confirmed the single pedagogical success I had notched up the previous day: When, after reading to them for half an hour from Ivan Kraus's humorous stories, I asked hoarsely for someone to take over from me, Agata's hand immediately shot up. Admittedly she didn't manage to control her breathing (let alone do any *voice work*) but she did read with unaccustomed conviction and even ticked off some of her less enthusiastic fellow pupils.

"Have you gone soft?" they flew at her.

"Not at all," Agata said elegantly and flashed me sweetly conspiratorial smiles.

By the end my jaw ached from *spontaneously* returning them.

During the next period I went to lunch.

When I was returning to my office, standing all along the corridor in regular intervals were sixth-year girls armed with damp cloths wiping every nook and cranny in the decorative posts of the cast-iron railing.

"Hello, girls. What are you up to, for heaven's sake?"

"We're dusting," Andrea whispered. "It's a practical with Mata."

"We're dusting for points," Jirina whispered.

"For points?" I said in surprise.

"It's daft, isn't it?" Andrea said softly.

"It is a bit," I agreed. "But why are you whispering?"

"We have to," whispered Jirina.

"What's going on down there?" Mata called from the upper floor.

The Principal turned up for the parents' conferences that afternoon in a splendid grey-blue suit, which - in the lingo of the pupils at our school - was almost *without fault*. (The only fault one could possibly find - and it really is a triviality - was the red piping down the side of the trousers and the visible inscription U.S. NAVY that remained on the right sleeve of the jacket.) The exceptionally well-fitting jacket, which incidentally was indirect proof that even an American naval officer can have a paunch, boosted the Principal's already considerable self-confidence to such a degree that he fielded the traditional critical questions during the parents' council meeting (*Why hadn't he submitted any proposals yet? Why was the school losing staff, and young teachers in particular? Why did the school have a subscription to* The Angler *magazine?*) with derisive nonchalance and triumphal references to *legal subjectivity and the*

78

widened powers of school principals. Apart from that, the parents' conferences followed their usual pattern: the parents, obliged by the cleaner to remove their shoes as they came in, stood in long lines on the linoleum in their socks and stockings in order to learn, after an hour of waiting for the teacher in question, that their adolescent child's main problem in life was an inadequate grasp of sulphates and oxides.

We don't want any great upheaval. There have been so many reforms already that they are black and blue from it. Petr Pitha

Elbowing my way along the overcrowded corridors, I kept my eyes lowered, so I almost missed Doubek's mother, whom I wanted to ask for advice on how finally to make her son *finish* the promised farewell speech - I tried explaining to her that the mere thought that I myself would once more have to draft the *thanks to the teachers* made me almost physically ill. She promised to *do what she could.* As we were saying goodbye, she wished me with a knowing smile *every success in my second job.*

The speed of data transfer in the Zbraslav local area network never fails to astound me.

"Thank you," I said. "But fortunately Mr Kral also pays me for my failures."

Only for my failures, I thought to myself.

We had agreed that he would wait for me in front of the school when the conferences were over. To my surprise, however, he was actually waiting for me in the office - seated on my own chair, one leg crossed over the other, drinking coffee from my cup and conversing casually with my colleagues.

"Hi there," I said guardedly. "It looks as if you are already acquainted."

"We've already been introduced," said Lenka and curtsied.

"Did you know Mr Nadany here used to teach me?" said Kral loftily as if that fact entitled him to certain privileges of some kind.

"Denis was my worst pupil ever," said Jaromir with a smile. "And I have to say, he did his very utmost to retain his pre-eminence."

Kral smiled at the compliment. Only now did I notice he had his shoes on.

"How did you get past the cleaners?" I enquired.

He pulled a handful of coins out of his pocket and jingled them cheerfully. "Like going through a turnstile."

I noted that he was capable of being quite witty (particularly when I write the repartee for him).

Reflections on the theme *footwear removal in Bohemia* were abruptly interrupted by colleague Trakarova, who burst into the staff room red in the face with indignation:

"Blinkered philistines! Petty bourgeois hypocrites!" she shouted about the parents.

In view of Kral's presence our expressions of agreement were that bit more ironic than usual, so a moment later she banged out of the room in a huff.

"She teaches sex education," I said, putting Kral in the picture. "I assume the parents have just barred her from doing *Venus Balls* with the kids.

"So how did you make out with the Principal?" I asked Kral in the car later.

"Child's play."

"What did he want? A taxidermy set? Or did he come right out and ask for a fishing punt?"

"Forty cages."

"*Forty cages*?"

He nodded curtly.

"There are thirty-six of us on the staff. I expect he wants four spares."

"Not at all," Kral laughed. "He wants them for his nutria."

The management of the V. Vancura Elementary School have once again provided convincing proof that they're not the kind of people who just grumble about lack of financial resources. The

Principal, Mr Naskocil, has come up with another innovative idea, namely: the purchase of a small number of nutria. These furry creatures with their highly prized pelts can be easily raised on the scraps from the school canteen, and the pupils will feed and look after them as part of their nature study and cookery lessons. The proceeds from their subsequent sale will, in the words of the Principal, be devoted to equipping a much needed computer room. As you can see, where there's a will, there's a way - even in our much criticised educational system. Well done! Zbraslav News, 8/1992, p. 2.

5. "I hate waiting," Beata said with annoyance. "I hate waiting for people I like - and I dislike even more waiting for the other sort."

She was slumped in the water chair. A bottle of wine stood on the floor next to the barrel.

"It really didn't occur to me that you might in any way miss my presence..."

"Who said anything about missing anybody?" she snapped. "I'm just saying that I really hate being kept waiting."

I was already familiar with this particular mood of hers: the need to argue was even stronger than her determination to stay silent.

"We had parents' conferences today," I said in a conciliatory tone. "We came straight from there."

"*Parents' conferences*?" she said mockingly. "Such things still exist?"

"They do," I said calmly. I looked at the closed curtains. "A lot of other things exist too. Such as *the sun*. Or *summertime*."

"And *hay*. And *strawberries*." She scowled: "You can stuff them up your arse!"

"Don't you find it tiring - having to play the demoralised cynic all the time?" I asked her. "Why don't you take a break from it for a moment?"

She was about to say something, but at that moment she noticed my tie. She leaned towards me in feigned amazement:

"What's that hanging round your neck, for God's sake?"

As she fingered it with distaste, I wondered to myself what had brought on this unwontedly communicative mood.

"*What's that?!*" she repeated in disbelief.

"Guess," I said patiently. "It's either: a) a common item of European male attire known as a tie, or b) my prolapsed colon - "

She giggled.

I gave her a friendly smile.

"And how about c?"

"C?" My eye fell on an open *Vokno* magazine. "An amulet to protect me from *cyberpunks*."

She immediately flared up:

"Kindly refrain from mentioning cybernetic punk because you don't know anything about it," she lambasted me.

"You're wrong there. When I wiped three months' work off my hard disk by mistake last year, my hair did a fairly good imitation of a punk *Chero* cut."

As she was just taking a drink, she spluttered wine over herself.

That made her fly into another rage:

"You know what you are: A pathetic *hack gagwriter*!"

A superficial humorist.

"Or do you really imagine that those *stories* of yours have anything to do with *real art*. I bet you've never even seen a *performance*. You've missed the boat. You're lagging fifty years behind."

"Behind whom? Behind what?"

She turned away from me in disgust.

With a sigh I reached for the aforementioned magazine to see whether there might be a chance of catching up a little with that boat of *real artists*. Performance, I read, is the art of displaying yourself. The aim is not simply self-expression, however. Anyway, the point is - in the European tradition at least - to preserve the artist's feelings for future generations. That is why it seeks to wake the public out of the lethargy of consumerism. It's not surprising that it has to choose techniques that shock, such as setting light to one's own body. Apart from self-ignition, Scott McLoad also goes in for riding on a conveyor belt and falling from it onto a

82

pile of coal. In short the artist/performer seeks new contexts - which can be a piece of polystyrene sheeting or a television set, for instance, which Marschall Weber uses in his performance to create a second head on his body. On the other hand, during the performance of Julie Regan and Ester Army Fischer, they fight like goaded animals to escape from a space surrounded by police barriers, constantly wounding each other in the process. In another performance, Ester plays a whore having intercourse with a lighted flame whose temptations she tries to evade (although tied to her left leg is the bowl in which, during the final cathartic scene, she burns her suspender belt while naked). The guitarist of *Tabor industrial group 3*, for instance, dances with an angle-grinder on a stage covered in empty fire extinguishers, which he goes on to touch with the angle-grinder; sparks fall onto the audience, who have no means of escape. One can also cover oneself in paint, of course, and fall on the ground, which incidentally enhances perception, or surround the stage with barbed wire, unwind oneself naked out of a sheet and bang one's head against corrugated iron. We are not talking about mere pictures, of course. What is shocking is the reality of it, which is a return to the fundamental sources and core of our being.

"I accept," I admitted at length, "that for years now in my chosen mode of writing I have been fundamentally in error."

She gazed at me warily.

"I don't know who was the cause of that dreadful error," I continued, "but in all events I'm deeply grateful to him for it."

She took a deep breath.

"You see I definitely don't relish the thought of book-signing sessions at which I'll have to burn my pen on a pile of coal or take off my clothes and deep-fry diskettes for my readers."

"Have it your way," she whispered angrily. "Let it be war, then."

I couldn't believe my ears.

"You have to be joking!" I said calmly. "If this has been *peace* so far, then I really would prefer war!"

VI

1. I was genuinely looking forward to the weekend at my parents' on the Sazava, as I was more in need of a rest than usual.

As for the weather, it fulfilled my expectations to the letter: from early morning a golden *sun* warmed the tiles on the terrace and the surface of the river; their neighbour contentedly turned the quickly drying *hay*, and every now and then my daughter would bring me fragrant scarlet *strawberries*. As soon as it was at all possible I tried, as I had resolved, to read, swim, devote myself to my family and not to think about Beata Kralova all the time.

Monday was the last day but one of the school year, and the general anarchy that reigned even before the first bell exceeded the most pessimistic expectations. During breaks one couldn't hear the sound of one's own voice anywhere in the school building, and even during the different lessons, the decibel level dropped only slightly. Not only did the usual chalks, blackboard erasers and plimsolls fly through the air, but also new textbooks and the ever popular exploding balls. Vladimir Havranek managed to fall into the street from a window in one of the sixth-year classrooms on the upper floor, although he escaped without the slightest injury, whilst the stoning of several pupils of the special school - traditional enemies - was prevented only by the timely intervention of members of the municipal police force. (I appreciate that authenticating such an accumulation of events might be a problem, particularly in view of the fact that the management of the school subsequently denied Havranek's fall from the window, and that for the life of me I can't find the cutting from the *Zbraslav News* confirming the attack on the pupils of the special school.)

As soon as he had completed the traditional morning ritual of tying fish hooks, the Principal subjected the situation, by then resembling a state of general emergency, to a thorough analysis, the conclusions of which could be best summed up in his own universal maxim: *no problem.* By contrast, the remaining pillars of authority, relying as they did for the rest of the year essentially on the threat of bad marks, reacted to the state of affairs by collapsing and swallowing tablets, venturing out of their offices only in the most urgent of cases - so that, paradoxically, the only one to spend that Monday morning at all peacefully was colleague Stribrny, who shortly before eight o'clock had been imprisoned by the ninth-year boys in the rather confined space of the *boxed vaulting horse*.

The essence of the teaching profession lies not in knowledge but in the personality, in what is most private and humanly intimate, in what links most firmly one person to another, even without words or scholarship: the art of human intercourse is the secret of success in training and education alike. Jaromir John

The Krals were flying off on holiday on Tuesday morning, so on the Principal's instructions the class teacher gave Agata her school report a day early.

That afternoon she showed it to me on her mother's insistence: she had three D's, one of them in language class.

"You're no good at Czech?" I said.

"Yeah, I know," she sighed. "Spelling."

"We'll have a go at it together when you get back," I said, looking at Mrs Kralova, who was washing the dishes.

"That would be very kind of you," Mrs Kralova said.

Agata merely smiled.

"That's if you want to," I added.

"Don't tell me you don't want to?" Mrs Kralova called.

On receiving no response from her daughter, she spurned her with a single wave of a wet hand. She then left the kitchen.

Agata was still smiling.

I couldn't help smiling too - I shrugged:

"All right then, we won't bother with spelling."

It was six o'clock.

"OK then," I said, rising. "Don't get drowned in the sea."

I ruffled her hair in a friendly gesture.

She seized me by the hand.

I looked at her in surprise, but she averted her gaze.

She kept holding on to me.

I looked towards the kitchen door in apprehension and urgently tried to think of something to say. But only a lot of stupidities came to mind:

How's Michael Jackson?

Have you got a pet animal?

Will you go collecting sea shells?

We give them rotten marks for Czech but don't know how to talk to them, I said to myself.

"Will you send me a card?" I asked her in a carefree manner.

She raised her eyes to me:

"And what about your wife?" she asked with genuine concern.

Beata had not forgotten about the declared war, unfortunately, (the fact that this was our last session before she left on holiday did not arouse in her any parting sorrow, unlike her younger sister). Her underlying combat strategy was tenacity. She maintained a glum silence, not reacting to anything at all. Not the slightest shadow of a smile escaped from her, and her unseeing gaze passed right through me with the skill of a downtown Prague waiter. Her most effective weapon, however, turned out to be the remote control of the Panasonic hi-fi tower: she would lie motionless on her stomach, the control unit hidden under her, allowing the room to fill with a heavy, stifling silence, before blowing it to smithereens in a split second, by an imperceptible change of pressure on the relevant finger. Those instant transitions from the total silence of the grave to the deafening infernal electronics of the group *Vanessa* had an oddly contradictory effect on my organism. In accordance with what I had read in the magazine *Vokno*, I felt on the one hand that my *resonating* body enabled me, *instead of merely consuming music, to become an integral part of it and that in this way I am linked electronically with all inhabitants of the global village known as Earth*, but on the other hand, a cold sore erupted on my upper lip, not to mention the fact that the giddiness I felt as I listened to it was not altogether unlike the feelings I had experienced years before at Pioneer camp when an earwig managed to creep into my middle ear.

At a quarter past seven I gave it up as a bad job.

"Have a good time!" I yelled into the thunder of metallic psychedelia.

Perhaps she did want to say something after all, because she immediately switched it off - but by then I was on my way downstairs.

"Enjoy the disco, then?" Jirik greeted me.

"Are you crazy?" I said jestingly. "Only an epileptic could stand that rhythm."

When Jirik had had a good laugh, he handed me the familiar white envelope: apart from five one-thousand-crown notes, it also contained a brief letter from Kral apologising for not having managed to say goodbye to me and informing me both about the date of their expected flight home and about his *firm conviction* that I was coping *truly excellently*.

I tell no lie.

2. Happily the graduation ceremony for teachers and pupils leaving the school for good at the end of the year went off in proper style - in the function rooms of Zbraslav Castle.

Shortly after nine o'clock these boys and girls standing on the very threshold of their lives were already standing around on the polished parquet floor and avoiding the stern gaze of the stone and bronze fathers of the nation. Even though their attire was in many cases a rather unsuccessful compromise between their parents' idea of formal dress and the fashion columns of *Bravo* magazine, they at least had clean hair, which in combination with the unwonted acquiescence with which they then formed themselves into the required three ranks, brought sentimental smiles onto the faces of their former teachers. Even colleague Andelova was smiling as

87

only an insignificant number of her pupils had headphones on their ears. Astonishingly enough, Irenka was smiling too because Zvara had not yet called any of those present a motherfucker out loud, and even colleague Stribrny was smiling, though his smile was not so much sentimental as an expression of his secret pleasure that he was separated from the ninth-year boys not only by a contingent of standard-bearing Zbraslav Scouts but also two rows of distinguished representatives of the *third resistance movement*. Last but not least there was even a smile on the face of Mayor Sopek who, before his speech, presented each of the assembled pedagogues with a single carnation in honour of their all-year-round *strenuous and responsible* work, and then - inspired most likely by the monumental patriotic sculptural group that towered behind him - went on to exhort the young people present to courage and great deeds (the young people, particularly the boys, applauded his words warmly, as several of them had some great acts of courage already in mind for the coming summer afternoon). To my surprise, however, the mayor went on to note that we were living in a period when education and people's creativity would determine the future of this civilisation to a degree unknown in any previous epoch, and that investment in education was in that sense capital on which the return might be slow but would be bountiful. Thus, he declared, it would be no exaggeration to say that any hesitation over investment in education could have fatal consequences. I gave him a look of sincere appreciation and was just about to make him a mental apology (while also fearing for his continued membership of the Civic Democratic Party) when he declared with equal conviction that the state could not invest in education, however, until it could afford to.

"That's dialectics, *comrade!*" I whispered in Jaromir's ear.

"We must save," said Jaromir, "whatever the cost."

"Shh," Vice-Principal Prochazkova admonished us.

Doubek deliberately avoided my gaze.

Mayor Sopka's speech was greeted with applause.

Yes, I know, another jolly scene. Do I really have to apologise each time?

For a very long time now we have tried legislating from the top down, with depressing results. It may profit us - even aesthetically - to reverse gears and try for a vulgar popularity. Walter Kerr, *How Not to Write a Play.*

The girls' choir, with their vigorous rendition of *It's a Long Way to Tipperary*, kicked off *The Little Garland of Songs* - so dubbed by colleague Chvatalova-Sukova, who had stood modestly throughout the mayor's speech beneath Myslbek's allegorical statue *Music*. There then followed *Deep in the Heart of Texas, One Man Went to Mow*, the surprisingly wanton *What Shall We Do with the Drunken Sailor*, and the obligatory *Auld Lang Syne.* The melancholic atmosphere of the closing composition: *Ach, synku, synku* (which, as the choir mistress rightly recalled, was T.G. Masaryk's favourite song) contrasted interestingly with Petr Doubek's vigorous onslaught.

"Hey Doubek, they said, it'd be great if someone thanked them or something. Thanked who? I asked. The teachers, who else? What for, I say, they get paid, don't they? But I kept on thinking about it. I don't say we shouldn't, I said to myself, but there's no need to go overboard. Well, I suppose you can say they taught me to read and write and the date of the Punic Wars and all that, but on the other hand I was kept in after school hundreds of times, got headlice five times, not to mention the fact that some nice individual stole my brand new gym shoes from the cloakroom - twice. I reckon we're about quits with the teachers, I said to myself. Anyway, we're packing it in in a couple of days' time, so why bother with thanks?"

The unprecedented unconventionality of this valedictory message caused a flurry of excitement amidst those historic surroundings - but happily also attracted rapt attention.

"But I couldn't get it out of my head," Doubek read. "I kept looking at the teachers, who were scarcely speaking any more and looked as worn out as the textbooks we were just handing back. So what? I said to myself, it's all part of their job description. In the end I sunk so low that I actually started to think about them - the teachers, I mean. The trouble is I still couldn't come up with

89

anything really suitable, except that I was getting a really weird feeling about it all - I'd only need to glance at that rubber plant that I'd brought to school in a yoghurt pot when I was in second year and see how it had grown right up to the ceiling and I'd get a funny feeling in the pit of my stomach. Or I put my foot on the cross-bar of Katka's chair, just like I'd always done, and all of a sudden I realised I wouldn't be doing that any more, and a lump came to my throat. God, you're not going to start crying, are you, you dumbo? I said to myself, and for some unknown reason I started remembering how my mother had a reunion of her old class last year. The Friday before, she bought herself a new skirt and nail polish in honour of it. On the Saturday she went to the hairdressers and spent the whole afternoon looking through old photos, and on the Sunday morning she announced to the family that she wasn't going anywhere because there are some things you just can't bring back - and I looked at the polished fingernails of the girls in our class and I thought of a load of questions but couldn't think of any answers."

At about this moment the first girlish sobs could be heard in the hall. "And then they came to see me again and said, haven't you got that speech ready yet, Doubek, for God's sake? - and I still didn't have it and I was just riled because in fact it was just another piece of homework that they'd given only to me and no one else. And I hadn't the foggiest idea what I was supposed to put in that speech, because it was obvious to me that if I wrote that our teachers gave us wings for our journey through life like the graduating class said last year, then Zeleny and Zvara would start waving their arms about and pretending to fly. One thing was clear to me - I'd have to write it in such a way that no one waves their arms about."

The sobs multiplied. A number of the boys cleared their throats in manly fashion.

"In the end, chance came to my assistance," Doubek said, excelling himself. "It was the day before yesterday. I was leaving the canteen after lunch and our class teacher called me over from the staff room window, and she called me Petr, in a natural way, instead of Doubek. I slowly went over to her at the window and wondered whether she had happened to see me drop that banana peel - and at that moment it came to me."

Doubek paused dramatically.

Veronika Pekarova burst into floods of tears.

"It struck me that in fact they had always been calling us. Calling us to come across the street, like my class teacher was calling me. Calling us to them, to the life of adults. It's true they talked to us about the Punic Wars, but at the same time they were actually calling us, not in words but just by standing there in front of us and giving us weary looks from time to time, as if to say isn't it time you stopped mucking about and flicking plasticine around and sailed across to us on the other bank. - And maybe it's that calling that we ought to thank them for."

The emotion that had seized many of the audience, including the teachers, even during Doubek's speech, was infectious.

Most of the girls were wiping their smeared eyes with paper tissues.

The lads chewed their gum stoically.

The community representatives whispered among themselves.

Etcetera.

When the group of well-wishers around Doubek finally started to disperse, I couldn't help following suit.

"A splendid speech," I said all of a quiver. "No one has ever said it to us so truthfully and sincerely. For years we've been waiting for that."

"Sorry about that," Doubek said reluctantly. "I wanted to write it, but I genuinely didn't manage it..."

3. About thirty hours later, I was setting off with my wife and daughter aboard one of Last Minute Travel's luxury coaches bound for the limpid Adriatic to launder Kral's dirty money in it.

We travelled the whole night. Despite the weariness caused by the previous days and unlike the majority of the other passengers, I was unable to sleep (not even with the help of the Sleepy-time inflatable cushion which my globetrotting grandmother had given me for the journey), and so, with the heightened attention of the wakeful I observed the red rear lights of the cars in front of us and later the rocky bulk of the Alps as they towered higher and higher above the brightly lit highway. As far as I recall, Macha didn't come to my mind. I pondered on all those girls I had suddenly been surrounded with, and from time to time I picked up my sleeping daughter's blanket when it fell on the floor.

A Czech teacher's family on the pier-head in Porec.

"Hello, sea," said my wife. "I don't know whether you remember me. It's nine years since we last saw each other."

"Hello, sea," said my daughter. "We've never met - my name's Misa."

The sea looked as if it couldn't care less.

One man said to the Universe:
Master, I exist.
The trouble is, the Universe replied,
that fact has not aroused in me
a sense of responsibility.

(I've forgotten who wrote that poem, but I had a similar experience with the Prague 5 District Education Office.)

Waves and salt in laughing eyes. Salt in the towels. Naked girls (who had anything but hateful expressions). The deceptive scent of suntan creams. Naked women. Inflatable mattresses. The boundary between light and shade at the edge of a pinewood. Books, baklava and Cézar brandy on an afternoon bungalow terrace. Lizards and cicadas. Warm nights. Scampi and Teran white wine in a restaurant lit with coloured lamps. Striped sailor's T-shirts beneath the waiters' jackets.

Etcetera.

A short cut is helpful in several ways. It relieves the monotony of familiar terrain. Walter Kerr.

On the seventh day, during an *optional boat trip to ancient Pula*, I entered one of the many goldsmith shops there, just a few hundred kilometres from that bakery in front of which an artillery shell tore eight people to shreds, and bought two really *delightful* little chains for my wife and daughter.

When we sailed back into Porec a few hours later, I found Petrik sitting on one of the red benches opposite the pier-head.

He was holding up some car keys and jangling them merrily.

Time's up, I understood.

Even so, I can't say I was not pleased to see him.

Beata's black Golf stood at the opposite kerb.

My wife followed the direction of my gaze, as she had learnt to do during the previous week on the beach.

"A friend of yours?"

In the meantime he had come over to us, so he introduced himself. The long journey had made practically no impression on his summer suit, but above all I marvelled at the transformation of which his vocabulary was capable when required. He conveyed to my wife Kral's *sincere regret* that he was obliged to deprive her *so rudely* of her husband's company for the last four days of her holiday, but he stressed that it was truly a *very urgent* matter. He then voiced the hope that my wife would not *take offence, if, on behalf of his boss,* he might be permitted to offer her *a small financial recompense.*

At last I discovered how much, as a husband, I was worth: two hundred and fifty Deutschmarks a day.

It struck me as not too bad.

He gave me half an hour to pack.

My wife came to me a little while later.

"Will you cope here on your own?" I asked.

She smiled.

I could see she had something on her mind.

"Did you enjoy it here with us?" she asked.

I looked up at her from the open suitcase.

She was still holding the two bank notes.

"It's lovely - all of this - now," she said. "But I wouldn't want it at *any* price."

"We're agreed on that, then," I said.

I kissed her.

The little gold chain glistened against her tanned neck.

"I just wanted you to know," she said.

They waved me off as if I were a sailor.

Petrik pressed a button to lower the roof. The wind ruffled my hair.

"What's up, then?" I said.

I had to shout slightly.

"Has something happened?"

"What should have happened?" he said baffled. "They came home early, that's all."

"Oh, I see," I said.

"The princess is bored," he laughed.

It was raining in the Alps.

4. And the rain stayed with us all the way home.

I spent the night telling jokes to keep Petrik from falling asleep at the wheel. He drove very fast so that even though we stopped twice for food, we were back in Zbraslav by five in the morning.

The public housing estate was deserted, wet and dismal. Tanned legs in white shorts seemed pretentious and out of place among the puddles. The coconut-fibre soles of my sandals were instantly sodden with dirty water. I put my case down in the hall and went straight to bed.

When I got up that afternoon, my mood had not appreciably improved. Switching on the radio did nothing to dispel my feeling of dereliction. I had a shower and then went round to the woman next door for the newspapers and the mail - but none of the three letters provided any evidence of the fact I was a writer. That capped my disgust.

I didn't want to go anywhere.

I didn't want to sit in the dark.

I didn't want to listen to a band called Vanessa.

At five I got dressed and went to see her.

The Krals weren't home. The house looked completely dead. Jirik was sitting in the kitchen with his forehead resting on the table top, snoring loudly.

Otherwise it was quiet everywhere.

I went straight upstairs.

The view that met my gaze when I opened the door of Beata's room was one I shall never forget.

The curtains were drawn.

The room was tidied.

A teddy bear was seated in the dentist's chair.

A school globe had newly appeared on the desk.

The barrel was covered by a white tablecloth, and on it stood a vase of ox-eye daisies.

On the wall facing the door hung a guitar and a poster of Janek Ledecky.

Beata was asleep on a bed - which had been *made*. Her washed hair was tied up with red ribbons into comically protruding little plaits.

Red also was the colour of her lipstick.

I leaned over towards those red lips.

The next moment the kitchen door banged downstairs, and the washing machine in the bathroom started to spin. There was the sound of rapid footsteps on the stairs, and Agata flung herself round my neck.

Beata opened her eyes.

"Hi there," she said. "We were beginning to miss you."

VII

1. "Well?" she said a moment later, after looking around her. "Does it suit your petty-bourgeois notion of a *young lady's bed-room*?"

For the first time ever I saw her smile for real.

"No. But it does suit my notion about the liberating effect of parody."

"And you, for that matter, suit my notion of a parody of Prince Charming."

I observed her with a certain amazement: a smile did undreamt of things with her face.

Her eyes suddenly sparkled:

"I bought you a present in Barcelona," she said with gratitude. "In a second-hand bookstore."

She handed me a small, carefully wrapped book.

"Pestalozzi," I conjectured. "Or Rousseau, perhaps?"

"Comenius," Beata said appreciatively. "You were close."

She was beginning to surprise me pleasantly.

She behaved with unwonted friendliness - even bringing herself to ask me in bourgeois fashion what sort of time I'd had. I told her a bit about Porec, Pula and Umag. She was full of goodwill and patently reluctant to argue, but when I mentioned the brightly painted little train linking Umag with the summer resort of Katoro, she was unable to control herself:

"A brightly painted little train?" she repeated my words mockingly. "Don't make me laugh."

"Yes," I said rather starchily. "A *brightly painted little train*. It runs about every twenty minutes. It's quite... practical."

"Jesus Christ! A *brightly painted little train*."

"What's wrong with brightly painted little trains?"

"Just the fact that it's utterly *phony.* Specious."

"So what?" I said, bristling to argue with her once more.

Argumentativeness, the last possible defence against desire.

"What has a brightly painted little train to do with *real life*?"

"What is *real life*?"

She made no reply.

"Stop your quarrelling," Agata said.

"You have in mind hospitals, divorce clinics, psychiatric wards and suchlike?"

"For instance."

"I live a real life the whole year long," I said. "The whole year long I go to work, go to funerals, breathe smog, visit my mother-in-law, look at the news... Can't I take a break for a week?"

She gazed at me with mute superiority.

"And how about you? What did *you* do in Spain?" I asked. "I assume that you founded an Anti-Cancer League at the very least..."

"She went to the bullfight," Agata said accusingly. "With an American."

I felt a slight stab of pain beneath my breastbone, but I laughed.

"Bullfighting *is* for real," Beata remarked.

"Give me strength," I said. "Now we have it: essence of Hemingway!"

"Were you ever at a bullfight?" she retorted.

"Never."

It sounded sharper than I had intended.

Suddenly she leaned over me:

"But you're *jealous*...," she said with unfeigned astonishment.

I changed the subject. First we chatted about furniture and living in general (I recall saying some nonsense like *every interior is the imprint of the human soul*) - and then I wanted Beata to tell me how her writing was coming along. She answered evasively.

"Have you written anything?" I asked directly.

She nodded.

"Will you let me read it?"

"No."

It sounded final.

"And what about our course?"

She did not reply.

"I'd only recall that I'm being paid for it..."

"Why don't you take a running jump with your fucking money!" she said fiercely, but on our way down to the kitchen, where Agata was making us a strawberry milkshake, she took a transparent green file out of the writing desk with a short two-page story entitled "Dad and I". As she handed it to me, I detected in her eyes a kind of bourgeois weakness.

"Thank you," I said.

She asked me to bring her my manuscript of *Those Wonderful Rotten Years* the following day.

Unbelievable.

Agata stayed with us in the kitchen. I had no wish to put her in her place in any way (and risk having her sulk for several days again), and besides, I had the feeling that her presence would help ease my conversation with Beata, which was still a bit uneasy at times.

This was how Kral found us on his return. It was still well before eight, so I was a bit concerned at what he would say about this untraditional approach to teaching. But when he saw the erstwhile high priestess of sorrow happily sipping a milkshake, he expressed intense satisfaction - and when Beata (to my not inconsiderable astonishment) presented a number of my earlier, more or less random comments about the advantages of skylights in terms of *our joint plan for the extensive reconstruction of her bedroom*, his joy at something so *constructive* knew no bounds. Wildly nodding in agreement, he called his wife in and joyfully described our plans to her. He sat bubbling over with ideas, repeatedly putting his arms round each of his daughters in turn. Eventually he rushed off to his office for his notebook from which he triumphantly read out to us the names, addresses, telephone and account numbers of *the best, speediest, and most reliable* building and furnishing companies in the Czech Republic. A moment later Agata got up, bored, and walked away, but Beata anxiously scrutinised my face - perhaps in search of the slightest hint of irony, but her effort was pointless as I would have been the last not to have appreciated the joy and relief that a sudden change from the spiritual to the rational could bring, or - in her father's case - the change from the thin ice of *metallic psychedelia* to the firm ground of *building inspection*.

"You could go to IKEA tomorrow," Kral mused out loud. "They've got some *lovely pieces* there."

"We're planning to," Beata declared. "Though the Professor here doesn't know yet."

"*When* tomorrow?" I said.

"Tomorrow *first thing*," Beata said with emphasis. "Daddy will pay you overtime."

We all laughed at that.

2. I was sincerely curious about Beata's story. I read it through at home that very evening (with a certain minor thrill, far removed from that *a priori* sceptical apathy with which - after a year of working in a publishing house - I pick up an unknown manuscript nowadays). I don't mean to pretend that the story is *crucial*, one that throws an entirely different light on Beata, but I decided to include it here because its refreshing realism came as a pleasant surprise to me after her hoo-ha about *real art*. Moreover, it seems to me interesting in many respects, and last but not least - in contrast to my many pages of second-hand references - it is one of the few truly authentic testimonies about the *tragically departed B.K.*

I have transcribed the story word for word, with just a few minor corrections of punctuation:

Dad and I

Going home, then? Mr Pospichal welcomes me from the steering wheel. So here I am again sitting in the bus on my way home. At my side a completely unknown guy with that arrogant checkered pattern on his trousers (I call it arrogant, because it always forces

*your eyes to follow those diverging lines), but it's all on account of
those incredibly inconsiderate seat reservations that permit a total
stranger to plonk himself down beside you without a word, and
open his incredible briefcase in a matter-of-fact way that deserves
a face-slap, and then to start leafing through an incredibly important diary (I just don't understand how, at the end of the twentieth
century, someone can put on a show like that with a totally straight
face!). Now, of course, he's shutting it again, the show's over, and
he can start to snore and (I assume) rest his head on my shoulder
and rub his horrible stubble against my sweater. Now, on top of
everything, he has calmly taken a sideways look at me; well, it
wouldn't have been so bad if he had looked, but he just blinked his
puffy eyelids and closed his eyes. I don't believe it - he's actually
snoring! In my presence.*

*Oh, thank God, here comes the village of my birth, the white
signboard with the black lettering, graphically terrible, but there's
scarcely time to notice it before here's the village square straight
out of "The Bartered Bride", and Dad, my Dad, in overalls.
Everything I used to love now seems so yokelish all of a sudden.
The guy next to me wakes up, so of course he sees this dump that
I'm getting out at. Hello there! Dad yells - why does he always
have to yell so loud? - and everyone in the bus can see him handing Mr Pospichal plastic bags full of frozen bulls' balls, and Mr
Pospichal gives Dad a big handful of Brufen - and now one of the
silver strips falls into his wellington boot and Dad - Oh, no, surely
not - takes it off and displays to all the passengers at the windows
of the bus those orange Chemlon socks that outlive your feet and
another strip falls right under the wheels and while Dad is bending
over near the tire Mr Pospichal playfully lets the clutch out slightly. Stop, you bastard! Dad yells and something goes in his back
and he straightens up with difficulty and Mr Pospichal calls to him
Take your Brufen, old boy! I look elsewhere. Hello then, Dad
eventually says, what's that you're wearing? and he looks at my
beret and my Paris jacket. But I can tell he approves. He kisses me
awkwardly and strokes me with a palm full of splinters from the
forest (once I actually got a splinter straight from his hand) and
he looks at me and all of a sudden I can tell he's sorry I quit the*

university. He took me there on the first day, through the park in front of the station. That was quite a nice part of the walk - those chestnut trees. Then I would always look up at the big flag in front of the Brazilian Embassy. But then came that horrible subway under the highway - but how can you tell someone you gave up university on account of the smell of urine in the subway - and all of a sudden he says, Veruna's getting married today. Didn't you know?

He opens the door of his new VW. Do you want to drive? he asks me and I look at the gear stick onto which he's screwed a varnished lump of natural wood and I say: I'm supposed to change gear with that? I might as well be digging out tree stumps... and Dad laughs and deliberately teases me, What do you think about that, then? pointing at the steering wheel that has a new calfskin cover, and I realise he wants me to be his clever, witty girl and so I say: Dreadful - did you really miss that old cow so much, the one you were still riding around on not so long ago? That's bollocks, Dad laughs happily. No way is it bollocks, I say, any psychiatrist would explain it to you. Psychiatrists my arse, my father laughs! I laugh but I'm tired. Don't you worry, Dad says, if those bastards buy that field, you'll get that Golf. I start to tease him about the dirt in the cassette rack, but he's already staring at the level patch below the village pump. What are they up to? he says, recognising them now. Oh, Zeman, he says. And his melody boys, I think to myself, a trifle wistful already. And his melody boys, Dad says, and I laugh. They've got us trapped, Dad says. Have you got any change? There's no way I'm giving them the big note: I pull out two hundred-crown notes for Veruna and her bridegroom. They're already stopping us. Every trip I make is a trap. Zeman has a checkered butcher's shirt - those arrogant checks again - someone is making me take a drink again. Again I'm having to smile when I don't feel like it. Again someone's looking sideways at me - my Dad, a stranger with the same seat reservation.

3. Next morning I brought Beata both her story and my manuscript, but I was disappointed to find she had no desire to talk about literature (I actually quite felt like starting the course in earnest).

Her mind was clearly elsewhere - I still don't fully understand how it happened, but that was how it was: Beata was totally absorbed with the idea of furnishing her bedroom. In a single night a stack of *Ideal Home* magazines, three feet high, had risen alongside her bed. It needed no more than a night for her to present her newly born idea of re-organisation as a plan she had always had but never achieved and for her vocabulary suddenly to include such expressions as *rhythm of form, natural light* or *lamella walls*.

"Lamella walls divide a room optically while also ventilating it," she would declare.

She said she had already been out for a jog and by chance had stopped just by the window of the local furniture shop. Most of the items on display were, she said, either the usual tacky housing estate stuff or those eternal *pseudo-rustic creations*, but apparently they also had an absolutely fantastic rocking chair in bent beech. On her way home she had given a bit of thought to curtains, hesitating, it seems, between a tender pink and a white harmony of *tone-on-tone*. I tried to damp down her enthusiasm (fearing, naturally, for its *lasting quality*), but the results of my efforts were paltry. Admittedly I did manage to persuade her that we should at least measure the room and draw a plan, but all my appeals for *conceptual reflection on possible variations of the interior design* (let alone my suggestion that we call in an interior designer) she dismissed with scorn.

"Why? What for?" she demurred. "Who's going to be living here, an architect or me?"

We arrived at the IKEA department store before it opened. We then spent the morning, in accordance with the list drawn up by Kral - which I held on my knee in the car like a route map, rally-driver style - visiting (if my memory serves me right) three other department stores, two antique shops, the shop that sells Danish Scaneco furniture, specialist carpet shops, several other shops selling cane, bamboo and wicker furniture, the Kratochvil and Triant shops, and the Europa Möbel warehouse (it occurs to me that I ought to point out that *none* of the firms mentioned in this book has sponsored its publication). In the space of those roughly four hours we bought a three-door wardrobe and three black-ash bookshelves, a set of black trolleys, two tubular armchairs with dusty-pink cushions in Thirties style, a dusty-pink long-pile wool rug, and a black Trend waste-paper basket. At the Dila art shop we managed to obtain a description-defying black glass object which from the very first moment repelled me because of its striking resemblance to an X-rayed squirrel while, by contrast, what attracted Beata was its *indefinability and its capacity to infinitely diffuse the light of so-called truth.*

The only things we failed to get were wallpaper with the desired pattern, a bed and a ceiling lamp.

The basic outline of the overall concept repeatedly insisted on by me was created by Beata in the car as we drove from shop to shop - and she gave it the final touches at the counter while rummaging in her handbag for her cheque book. My role mostly consisted of vain attempts to measure a particular item before Beata paid for it - for which I was rewarded on the way home by her generous offer to let me choose anything I could make use of from the original furnishings. The thought that I might incorporate half an oil barrel in the inventory of our bourgeois living room brought a smile to my face.

Beata took umbrage and stepped on the accelerator.

"I'd love to take the dentist's chair," I said hastily.

In spite of my wife's occasional (though fortunately, with the passage of time, increasingly ritualistic) protests, it continues to stand in my study, locked in a position that actually invites meditation. The original light-coloured hygienic leatherette having been rather worn and also torn in a couple of places, I asked my furrier grandmother to sew me up some kind of loose cover; thanks to the fact she used leather scraps of various colours, the chair has lost its severe aspect, so that I have even had visitors who have been unable to guess its erstwhile drastic purpose. (Besides, it's something I do myself, *i.e.*, sew cheerful loose covers to mask the naked pain of reality.)

103

On her return from Prague, Beata carried out a lightning inspection of her room. Then she went straight to the telephone to tell her father how amazed she was that although it was already one o'clock in the afternoon, her apartment did not *yet* have the required skylights - Kral apparently promised her immediate redress because by the end of the conversation she was unambiguously smacking her lips into the mouthpiece.

Being a grass widower, I accepted with gratitude an invitation to lunch.

Agata spilt only one glass.

After lunch, Beata changed into her working clothes (a black Japanese kimono with a dragon on the back, and a silk headscarf), and we set about clearing out the bedroom.

On the stroke of three, a delivery van from the firm of Velux drove through the front entrance. Five men in matching red overalls carried tools, stepladders, planks, window frames, panes of glass, roofing material and fibreglass up to the loft, and their subsequent hammering made the house literally uninhabitable. Beata decided that the time we had to spend outside would be used for burning *old junk*, by which she meant several wooden crates, hidden till then beneath her bed. While Petrik helped us carry them outside, Agata lit a fire in the old fireplace in the garden.

Beata opened the smallest crate, which mostly contained souvenirs of November 1989: hand-painted banners with the words *Who, if not ourselves? When, if not now?* and *Truth again tomorrow morning*; a strip of cloth announcing the continuing strike at the Radotin grammar school, dried orange peel, crumpled pieces of tricolour ribbon, photos of Vaclav Havel, Valtr Komarek, Milos Zeman and Cardinal Tomasek, plus several badges with the text *Dubcek for President*. She rummaged among them with evident distaste, tossing out something here and there, but in the end she tipped the whole crate into the fire.

Now I would go through fire and water for our President, but at that moment, pulling his photo out of the flames seemed a bit excessive. Petrik grinned cheerfully.

"Stolen revolution?" I remarked for Beata's benefit.

She brushed it aside as not being worth answering. It was *passé*.

By contrast, the contents of the second crate had a powerful effect on her. She picked up yellowing drawings and crumpled magazine cuttings with emotion and affectionately pulled out - and read - some typewritten poems or other. She carefully untied letters bound up with a faded ribbon, gazed mutely at photographs of young men (who definitely did not manage to get into politics), sniffed a champagne cork and caressed a Sparta ice-hockey shirt with the number 22. Her kimono had the effect of making me feel at times I was in a film drama by Akiro Kurosawa.

"I'm going to make myself a coffee," I said.

"Wait." She seized me by the arm.

With the expression of someone severing all ties, she threw into the flames her certificate for coming second in the district cross-country championships and a pillowcase stamped *Hotel Krivan*. This only reinforced my initial impression that she had no real desire to burn her past, but only to exhibit it.

Then, like a sleepwalker, she thrust a sort of photograph at me:

"That's him..."

The Looney, I realised.

I pondered on his singular expression - his face looked almost as if he had just swum the Channel both ways, while despising swimming, the Channel and photography. When I turned the photo over, I discovered on the other side transcribed in pencil a poem by Ginsberg about the firm bottom of some dead baseball player.

I threw it in the fire; little brown blisters erupted on it before the heat suddenly contorted it.

Agata glanced in shock at Beata.

She was as white as a geisha but said nothing.

Petrik looked on with interest.

I threw in a few other items. The Sparta shirt and the Krivan pillowcase burned badly.

"Want it to burn *properly*?" asked Petrik.

"Let's give him the job," I said to Beata. "I expect he has plenty of experience burning incriminating materials."

He laughingly dowsed the smouldering remains, tossed them back in the crate and ran off to the garage. In less than a minute he was back and spent a moment fiddling with the crate. I led the two sisters some distance away.

Beata walked a trifle stiffly but made no resistance.

"Hold on to your hats," Petrik said with relish. "It'll make a bit of a bang."

"Krakatit," I said.

I put my arms round the girls' shoulders and used my body weight to pull them to the ground.

Their hair smelled of smoke.

Only a tuft of grass separated me from Beata's face - I was a trifle embarrassed at this as my enlarged pores are visible from close up.

Beata Kralova's past exploded in a fiery ball of petrol vapour.

And that was that.

4. The second shopping day was one of *encounters*: even though the holiday period was far from over, we managed to bump into several acquaintances in the course of our short walks around the centre of Prague.

The first such meeting occurred in Dlouha Street, and apart from anything else was a lesson that you can't get rid of your past just by burning a few letters and photographs.

"Buddha!" Beata exclaimed joyfully.

This hitherto living part of her past had a beard down to his waist, an embroidered sweat-sodden shirt unbuttoned as far as his mighty belly and unbelievably dirty bare feet in leather thong sandals.

"Little Beata! Flower of the desert!" exclaimed the last beatnik of central Prague. "Quick, come and kiss my beard."

He slobbered all over her, but she seemed to enjoy it for some unknown reason.

"Whither are you blowing, little breeze?" he marvelled. "Where will you fall, little leaf?"

She hesitated:

"We're just out for a walk..."

"Walkies, eh?" he laughed enigmatically. Walky walkies?"

"Of course" said Beata. "Ordinary walkies."

"We're looking for wallpaper," I added helpfully. "And a lamp."

He made a face as if I had spoken in Finnish, and with the horrified expression of a huge goblin who had wandered into the middle of a tennis match by mistake, gazed back and forth between Beata and me.

"You don't say!" he eventually said in amazement.

Beata exhaled smoke.

"Of course," she said mystically.

"Five big smackers, eh?" he said knowingly. "So some shinies, then?"

"What do you think?" Beata said pointedly.

For the first time he turned to me:

"Some real shinies, eh?"

I glanced briefly at Beata, but she looked away.

"Of course," I said at last, judging that I would have as much difficulty saying the word *shinies* as I would giving the order *Line up, 8C*.

He continued to peruse me:

"Shiny shinies?"

He gave a knowing wink.

I had had about enough.

"I suppose so," I said wearily. "I suppose that might be the slang expression for it."

He stepped back slightly and brought his face close up to mine. Then he backed away:

"What sort of a shit-head is that you're dragging along with you?!"

I introduced myself.

"Who's that shit-head?!" he blurted uncomprehendingly.

Beata mutely stroked his sweaty temple.

"We won't delay you further," I said. "Besides, I suppose you'll be hitch-hiking off somewhere, won't you?"

Beata laughed, and actually looked at me.

It was nice.

"What fucking hitch-hiking? What kind of a fucking shit-head is that?" he yelled at her frustratedly.

"In that case I expect you'll be rushing off on some *rave* or other?"

He heaped on me a series of oaths.

The pleasure was mine.

At the carpark on Charles Square - still without a lamp, but by now loaded down with a dozen rolls of wallpaper - we encountered David Sulc, a civil engineer as well as a family friend and fellow pupil of mine from grammar school. I introduced him to Beata with a certain degree of satisfaction as the feet in *his* leather sandals were clean. I described Beata as a friend of mine.

"Where are you and your friend off to?" he enquired.

"My friend and I are looking for a ceiling lamp," I told him cautiously.

He nodded understandingly, without feeling any need to comment further.

He couldn't have chosen any better way at that particular moment to strengthen our friendship.

"And a bed," Beata added. "My writer friend is helping me choose it - he truly is an expert on beds..."

She gave me a grateful peck on the cheek and sighed.

I couldn't help noting silently that our mutual duel had entered a rather dangerous, albeit extremely pleasant, phase.

David nodded rather sadly, jutting forward his chin slightly (a gesture of resignation I had last seen him make a few years previously on the Sazava, when I quite unexpectedly beat him at ping-pong).

"Perhaps I ought to have gone in for writing, too," the engineer said pensively.

Third time unlucky was in Zbraslav when, at Beata's insistence, we pulled up in front of the furniture shop *just on the off chance* and bumped into my colleague Tauferova.

"This *fantastic woman* is Beata Kralova?" she exclaimed in disbelief.

She had taught her in Russian class years before.

She complimented Beata on her *beautiful* summer dress and her *beautiful* tan and gave us an extensive report on the health of an old aunt of hers who had leukaemia. She then expressed an interest in what we were carrying; she pronounced the sample of the wallpaper bought to be *very pretty,* and the paste chosen to be *excellent.*

In the end her restraint gave way:

"And where are your girls, then?" she *recalled.*

"Still at the seaside," I said calmly. "I had to leave earlier because of a job."

She smiled a lipstick smile.

"Send them my regards, then."

5. The speed and degree of organisation with which Beata's room was refurbished, not to mention the number of workers involved, recalled the construction of the set for a big-budget American film when the producer is trying to beat the clock - the installation of both skylights was completed that same night. The next morning the wallpaper was on the walls and the room was tidied ready for the employees of Slejchrt and Son, Flooring Contractors to lay the pink pile carpet after lunch. So there remained nothing for Agata, Beata, Petrik and me to do except to carry up to the bedroom at a leisurely pace, first the original furniture and then the newly purchased items in the order in which the different shops delivered them during the afternoon. I must say that in spite of the previously mentioned differences between Beata's taste and my own, in the end the room as a whole (even with the old bed and without a ceiling lamp) looked surprisingly agreeable and cosy - and when, to boot, I had carried out the oil barrel, which was still blocking the mezzanine, and placed it under the drainpipe of the Krals' garage, I couldn't help feeling that my optimistic, rationalising mission had not been entirely unsuccessful.

Mr and Mrs Kral arrived shortly before seven. They came just as I was completing the systematic arrangement of Beata's books in the new-smelling bookshelves (in the process of which I intuitively combined the *national* approach with a criterion which I defined as *the author's degree of freakiness*), and at the very moment when, with the help of some fragmentary knowledge of Freud, I was trying to explain the girls' joyful humming as they tidied Beata's panties and bras away into one of the compartments of the new black wardrobe. The soft light of early evening shone through the skylights, suffusing the pink of the carpet with a warm, golden glow. Kral took off his shoes:

"Fantastic!" he declared with conviction.

Mrs Kralova stroked my hand and told me it was a *fairy story*, and that I was a *born magician*.

I understood what she meant - and with a kind of *cheerful modesty* I strove in vain to make one serious point: that these days, unfortunately there was not just one evil giant that could be conveniently dispatched; and that the dragon sometimes had more heads than we could cut off.

In his socks Kral crossed over to his daughters and kissed them.

Then, ignoring my half-hearted protests, he dragged me off to his office, where he awarded me a virile embrace, a glass of Glen Deveron scotch and ten thousand crowns.

"I knew you'd manage it," he said with emotion.

VIII

1. When Beata and I went back upstairs again after dinner, it was already dark outside. As a result, we discovered that one of the advantages of a skylight is the possibility of observing the night sky without moving from one's room. So we sat down on the 1931 armchairs and stared at stars that were millions of years old.

"Fantastic," I said.

Our sudden discovery inspired Beata to a number of time-space reflections that I am incapable of reproducing here even approximately (I recall only her assertion that it could be a way of understanding *absolutely, but absolutely everything*, which triggered off in me the irrational hope that from this position I might one day understand even the novels of Daniela Hodrova).

"Surely one need not understand everything," I commented in accordance with my conviction and went on to inform her, *inter alia*, about Vonnegut's term: *protection from information*.

"A protector from information," she mused. "That's a censor."

"A *self-censor*," I stressed. "There's a difference. One deliberately and voluntarily avoids *certain* information - in the interest of one's own mental health."

"And lies to oneself."

"And *mercifully* embellishes reality to render it more bearable."

"Viz that novel of yours," she said suddenly.

My pleasure at the speed with which she had read it was tempered by a fear aroused by the very expression: *that novel of yours*.

"Go on," I said bravely.

(*An artist does not need criticism, an artist needs praise. When he needs criticism, he's no artist.* Gertrude Stein)

"Isn't it one and the same thing?" she nodded her head from side to side: "That constant obsession with *entertainment*..."

111

I shrugged:

"It's a fear of being boring."

She scowled:

"Doggies, grannies, budgies... do you really need such things?"

I took the liberty of reminding her reproachfully of certain key principles of my aesthetic that I had explained to her during our first lesson, and after going over that old ground I went on to acquaint her with my favourite parallel, one that I had not yet used, in which my writing is compared to a frontline soldier's letters to his mother:

"You see," I explained, "there he is with all the flak whistling above his head, while down below the bedbugs and rats are making a meal of him, and he is so hungry he could even eat the guts of his closest comrade hanging on the barbed wire over there - but each time he writes home to his mother that he is well and that he'll come home soon..."

"Because in my view that lying version is his sacred duty," I added with a certain fervour.

"You've lost your temper," she noted.

I told her that as a sort of voluntary liaison officer between scorned reading matter that people bought and literature that was respected but read by almost no one, I naturally have to expect being called nasty names by both camps from time to time. I hoped that she would show due appreciation for my brilliant exposé, but by then her thoughts were evidently elsewhere.

"When would you *definitely* kill yourself?" she asked out of the blue.

The immediate switch from a conversation about my novel to considerations about my possible suicide amused me.

She insisted on a reply, however.

"I would definitely kill myself if I tried to use an oxyacetylene welder."

She told me reprovingly to give a serious answer.

I thought about it.

"Definitely? If my daughter were to marry someone *really dreadful*..."

"Like who?"

112

"Like Pavel Vitek," I said. "Or Buddha."

I shuddered theatrically.

"*Wisecracks*," she said sadly. "You see? You're not even *capable* of speaking seriously any more."

"They're not wisecracks. It's what Romain Gary talked about - a way of neutralising reality when it's about to go for your throat."

"Wisecracks and *quotations*," she added disappointedly.

She yawned.

I stood up.

"I propose a truce," I said. "Let's set aside our different philosophies of life - and let's stay friends."

"Shall we go and get that lamp tomorrow?" I asked on my way out (something prevented me from uttering the word *bed*).

She burst out laughing.

That was typical: if I had stood in the door and asked her about Toyen or Sartre or the history of Christianity, she wouldn't have batted an eyelid. I ask her about a lamp - and she almost bursts a blood vessel.

"We'll go first thing in the morning," she said with eyes full of happy tears. "You can sleep here if you like."

Beyond the skylight leered the faces of fake gardeners, looneys, Barcelona Americans and Sparta hockey players.

"There's a job I still have to do at home," I said in strangled tones.

2. Today Ota Karlas brought me the proposed designs for the covers of the New Czech Prose titles for this year. In the spirit of the general editor's requirements, they are plain and unadorned; just bold black type on a monochrome background. Eva Kanturkova's *Memorial* was yellow, Lubomir Martinek's *Cape of No Hope* blue.

"I'm reserving a pink one," I told Ota. "It's going to be a *love story* with all the trimmings."

He bestowed on me one of his genial smiles.

I awoke to a magnificent sunny morning. I had breakfast, picked up the folding ruler and after complaining solely for form's sake about *this style of summer*, I joyfully rushed out of the house.

Contrary to my expectations, we weren't to go for a bed or for a ceiling lamp, but - as Agata in a blue swimsuit called to me from the terrace - for a swim. She waved to me and disappeared inside the house.

"For a swim?" I said to Beata, who was washing the windshield of the convertible.

"At Slapy," she said imperiously.

Agata - in a green one-piece swimsuit with large white dots - was already bringing blankets and a wicker hamper.

"I don't have my swimming trunks," I pointed out.

"We'll lend you Dad's," Beata said, nodding to her sister, who ran off again laughing and returned with them a moment later wearing a gold bikini that comically exposed her skinny little bottom. Beata raised her eyes heavenwards. I wanted to help Agata overcome her embarrassment (and spare us a further change of costume) so I forced myself to wolf-whistle appreciatively. She blushed with pleasure and wanted to give me a playful slap, but as she brought back her arm, she banged her hand on the rear-view mirror:

"Ow!"

Beata raised her eyebrows and straightened the mirror.

She put on dark glasses.

"Well," she said amiably, "do you think we can go now?"

The road was empty.

Beata drove swiftly but surely.

(I fear that from a certain moment the cliché *woman driver* lost any of its would-be humorous connotations for me, and these days, rather than a pretext for a silly joke it tends to represent a bewitchingly fascinating fusion of eroticism and death - which, I stress, is no intellectual pose.)

But on that occasion, it didn't yet.

On that occasion, the wind, still warm, ruffled our hair and washed over our faces. On that occasion, my inner sense of well-being was marred solely by the fact that Kral's trunks had a leopard pattern.

At the first straight section of road I lightly touched Beata's bare thigh with my finger and with my other hand pointed at the radiant ball of the sun:

"Shinies, eh?" Because of the wind I had to shout slightly. "Shiny shinies!"

The corners of her mouth betrayed her.

At Davle, Agata demanded an ice cream. We watched in amusement from the car as she stood in the short line bashfully hitching up her gold bikini bottom at regular five-second intervals.

"I treated you terribly," she said suddenly.

The face she turned towards me wore an oddly rueful expression.

I felt I understood her.

"I'd like to apologise."

She actually took off her sunglasses.

Changing into swimming things.

How to describe physical desire truthfully and convincingly while avoiding lurid pornography? Admittedly, in the era of *Penthouse*, sex columns, and louche songs with nationwide popularity I shouldn't need to get too worked up about excessive scruples, but I still can't entirely rid myself of qualms. I did have a couple of timid erotic passages in my previous novel, it's true, but in it I remained concealed (with the pleasure of a genuine voyeur) within the character called Guy, and besides, I could always get out of it by referring to the novel's fictional nature. But what can I do *here* in a chronicle of avowedly real events? Am I really, in the very next chapter, before the eyes of my daughter, my wife, my mother and my grandmothers, to unzip my fly and slide my bold rubicund lodger into the moist passage of twenty-year-old Beata Kralova? For God's sake!

How does that Vaculik do it?

After the rain of the previous days, the grass at Zdan was lush and the water was not tepid, as it often is here, but had a pleasantly cool sparkle. The morning fell into a fairly regular pattern of two alternating periods. When all three of us went swimming together, it inevitably involved Agata's usual screeching, splashing and underwater frolicking which caused the water literally to bubble. (Beata kept out of the way but Agata kept on clasping me ever more shamelessly with her skinny legs until - with the feigned crabbiness of an old leopard - I was obliged to hold her head under the water with my heavy paw just long enough to send her wading back to shore, choking with annoyance and with her eyes full of tears.) However, the times when Agata didn't feel like going in the water or had run off to find a friend, the mirror-like surface of the water hardly stirred when Beata and I cut through in two meticulously parallel paths. The pattern was similar on the shore also - as soon as we were left to ourselves on the blanket, the jolly banter quickly abated. The first time it happened, we lay there silently for a moment and then she asked:

"Do you celebrate New Year?"

I took her rather untopical query to be no more than a pleasing openness, a kind of teasing admission that she too was aware of the oppressive silence that had descended on our blanket after Agata's departure - but to my astonishment it seemed that she was genuinely interested. I therefore classified myself as somewhere between an orthodox enthusiast of champagne and fireworks and a no less orthodox disparager of New Year revels of any kind.

"Hm," she said. "And what do you think about when you wake up in the morning?"

I restored the quarter-inch gap between our sun-warmed shoulders.

"On New Year's morning, you mean?"

"On any morning," she explained. "I just want to know what you are thinking about when you wake up..."

I agitatedly summoned up the the most recent of the hardcore films that some unknown lecher had been projecting onto my retina each morning in recent days, films in which Beata played a role usually designated in theatrical jargon as a *juicy part*.

"Nothing out of the ordinary," I said. "It takes me a long time before I start ticking over. I'm not up to profound thoughts in the morning."

Beata's remaining questions - the ones I remember, at least - concerned my feelings about our national history (I think I described them as mixed), my expectations as regards the imminent age of Aquarius (ambiguous) and the reasons that had led me to choose the teaching profession (I told her I had always felt an intrinsic need to convey to others the exhilarating message of learning and pass on the baton of civil humanity, besides which I was in desperate need of an apartment). That brought us to the subject of marriage: How long have I been married? As long as that? Do we have friends in common? What does my wife do when I'm writing? How did we meet? Do I wash the dishes? What's the most difficult thing in marriage? What is the cause of divorce?

"Marriage," I said.

I had read it somewhere.

I did endeavour, nevertheless, to answer her as truthfully as possible, so much so, in fact, that I started to worry whether I hadn't created in her twenty-year-old eyes a picture of some dreadful *bourgeois* outlook - but she commended me on not trying on her that pathetic trick of *my wife doesn't understand me*.

"*My wife understands me* is just as much a trick," I pointed out.

"I know," she said mournfully.

Beata's questions... The closer we became the more there were. It would need an extensive and painstakingly classified subject index to plot them all, and an experienced psychiatrist to analyse them. She asked about everything from Apollinaire, Biedermeir, celibacy and Drtikol to xenophobia, yellow fever, Yellowstone Park and Zen Buddhism, and she could scarcely conceal her disappointment when I was unable to answer many of them.

Do I also feel *insincere* when I'm helping blind people across the road?

Do I also have moments when I hate *absolutely everyone?*

Do I know of any reliable *anti-stress* exercises?

Do parlour games *bore me to death* too?

What do I really think about Fucik?

Is *sexism* a myth?

Do I also feel like Mary Pickford when I'm in church?

Do I also cry sometimes when I'm watching children skating?

Do I also find the word *menstruation* really disgusting?

Do I also find so-called *conversation* really disgusting?

Do I also prefer *older* people?

Do *sad* people strike me as more truthful?

Am I going to meet the bus tomorrow?

Just like that. Without any link.

It was the afternoon before we had lunch - in town. We found a ceiling lamp. Our car was towed away. Beata laughed. She said it was two years since she had taken the Metro. Kral also laughed. He made a telephone call, and two hours later they brought the car back. Whilst I didn't join in the applause which Kral garnered, I did not feel sufficiently scandalised, however, at this direct proof of the existence of corruption in our fledgling democracy. My civic vigilance was waning.

I slept at home, though.

3. The Last Minute Travel coach was very late arriving because of a delay at the Italian border. I took advantage of the wait and my increasing nervousness to remind myself of certain enduring values which had underpinned my life until then.

Two hours later the coach finally pulled up at the kerb.

The hydraulic doors hissed.

When I eventually spied my wife among the crowd of tanned strangers, I noticed - rather to my surprise - that she was still pretty.

"Daddy!" my daughter called.

The little chain glinted on her brown neck.

One night, about a month after the beginning of my national service, I sat at the little metal table of the assistant duty-officer of the Bratislava-Vajnory regiment and wrote a *poem* about my relationship with my daughter. I take the liberty of quoting it here even though the very fact of having gone against my long-standing resolve and left the terra firma of prose in order to launch myself into the cosmos of poetry is a fairly eloquent testimony to my utter emotional unbalance at the time:

My daughter
never stops bothering me
and clinging round my neck
so I suffocate
when she's not there
to cling to me...

I think I'd better get back to prose:

Even though I apologised to Beata for my inadvertent delay and even though the old (*green!*) couch looked more than a little odd in the newly furnished room, she had no wish to go into town - she told me she was beginning to be *embarrassed* about *looking for a bed*. It took quite an effort on my part to convince her that it would be a pity to give up now and not put the finishing touches to it.

"Anyway it's too late," she said sulkily.

"It's mid-day," I objected. "We've plenty of time."

I couldn't rid myself of the feeling that her imagination put a rather different gloss on those two hours I had spent that morning walking about among the cigarette ends on the pavement of Opletal Street.

I eventually persuaded her - but all my previous efforts immediately came to naught in the very first furniture store we visited that afternoon. The manager's vulgar jocularity was incredible: conspiratorial winks, double entendres and a kind of louche indulgence, such as when he invited us to *try out straightaway* the beds on display. I simply treated him to several cold, pained looks, but the one who found his pressure impossible to bear in the end was, surprisingly, Beata - she sank listlessly onto the highly praised

119

double divan, white in the face and with her lips tightly pursed. Her every movement was accompanied by a frightful rustling from the plastic cover.

"How's that one for a good roll?" the manager boomed.

Instead of replying, Beata shut her eyes.

"Ecstasy - it was agony," said the manager.

I sat down by her on the edge of the bed.

She felt for my hand and squeezed it firmly.

"A bit of all right!" the manager whinnied.

He leaned over to look up her skirt.

"I think we need a stiff drink," I said.

She immediately squeezed me harder.

Her eyes remained shut even when I was leading her out of the shop and into the street to the accompaniment of the obscene comments of that idiot which were by then totally unambiguous.

After three cognacs in the restaurant bar at the top of the Kotva department store, she tried every bed in the furniture department on the floor below, spontaneously but with a certain solemn ceremoniousness: coloured double divans, the traditional *white bedroom*, modern iron bedsteads with brass knobs, folding sofabeds and even the circular marriage beds covered in American micro-plush.

She lay down on them with dignified concentration.

She turned over onto her side, her back and her stomach.

From time to time she fondled the upholstery.

She breathed on the headboard mirrors.

She cuddled several cushions.

She tested the softness of mattresses with her fingertips.

In the comfortable, black-upholstered *Wendy* bed costing 18,990 crowns she actually started to purr gently.

I chided her good-naturedly, falling in with her playacting.

"I want this one," she said.

"It has an adjustable under-pillow section and a removable mattress with down insert," the sales assistant said with pleasing matter-of-factness. "The cover is detachable."

She waited for Beata to get up and then demonstrated how to detach that sort of cover.

Beata linked her arm in mine:

"Do you see that?" she said tenderly. "Isn't it incredibly *practical*?"

"It has a large storage space," said the assistant.

She demonstrated it.

There was cognac on Beata's breath.

"A large space - did you hear that?" she said tenderly. "Isn't that so incredibly *optimistic*?"

Beata's touch was too pleasurable for me to go off and measure the bed.

"We'll take it," I said, rather mesmerised.

She gave me a long kiss as if I really had paid for it.

"I want to buy you some trousers," she whispered, when she had drawn breath. "Or a suit. Now. Straightaway."

It can't be helped, that was the way it was - no spring meadow in flower, nor even a borrowed country cottage with a roaring fire; instead, a cramped changing cabin in the men's clothes department like in the worst blue movie.

The unrelenting chink in the curtain when it was drawn.

Two overhastily chosen suits on the hanger.

The suspicious whispers of the sales assistants.

The big mirror of my moral turpitude.

And then, dear Gran, I kicked off my trousers and Beata stuffed her panties into her handbag.

"How does that fit you, sir?"

My wife commended my suit - and told me I'd done the right thing to buy it.

She said I had been needing something of the sort for ages.

Incidentally I wore it to the reception in Prague Castle to mark the founding of the Republic, as well as to the pre-Christmas meeting of artists with the ex-Minister of Culture, the recent writers' suppers at the American Embassy and, alas, to that gala evening to mark the beginning of the International Year of the Family.

...to steer the pupil into a relationship with the world; to awaken and develop his creative capacity to relate to the world. Otokar Chlup, Jaromir Kopecky and team, *Pedagogics.*

4. It was more than joy.

It was joy and fear simultaneously.

Fear that it would end.

Fear that it wouldn't end.

I really do not intend, in 1994, to prolong my Reflections on Love (note, for example, that in pragmatic fashion I do not regard the foregoing *act of penetration* as sufficient reason for starting a new chapter), but I must still at least admit that something really did change.

I started doing morning exercises.

I would take advantage of even the briefest of sunny periods to *feed* my Adriatic tan.

I pulled the hairs out of my nose with tweezers.

I bought five new pairs of underpants, five pairs of socks and (for the first time ever) tooth floss.

I stopped calling Updike's novel *Marry Me* "banal but pleasing overall".

Tears would spring to my eyes on hearing well-worn songs sung to a guitar by the weekend crowd on the Sazava:

I'll secretly cut a strand of your hair

To put under my pillow, fool that I am...

Oh Jesus! I would sob.

I'd never heard anything truer in my life.

At home things were really *terrible*. In my memory, the time I spent with my family during those first days is enveloped in a mist almost as if in a novel. All I know is that I zealously organised holiday outings (I recall, for instance, that we were at Konopiste, but I can't remember anything else - was the park closed?). Fortunately they didn't notice anything untoward - I had had moments of absentmindedness in the past also.

"Daddy's *writing*," my wife would explain indulgently to our daughter.

But that new secret permeated my entire body and filled it so entirely that it seemed inevitable that it would surface at any moment. My struggle to keep it inside at all costs caused my hands to start trembling. I knocked over and broke more glasses and cups than Agata. My intense efforts not to inflict hurt transformed me into a slave of conspiracy. The more letters I received from her, the more difficult it became to find a safe hiding place for them. I used to get up in the night and check my hiding places. If I had a yearning to see at least a photo of her, I would have to pull out Grandma's old dresser from the wall.

In spite of all those precautions I occasionally did find myself in unexpected situations where disclosure seemed totally unavoidable. Gentlemen, have you ever blown your nose abstractedly during a visit to your mother-in-law and detected in your handkerchief the unmistakable, intimate scent of your mistress?

Happily I soon found an absolutely reliable hiding place for the drafts of my own love letters (and *poems*, believe it or not): I gradually filed them in a folder on which I printed in large letters *LOVE LETTERS AND POEMS* - and stuck it into the pile of notes for my next novel.

They couldn't have been safer in a bank vault.

If anyone suspected anything, then it must have been our dog, which I took on unwontedly frequent walks. The moment I was out of sight of our windows I would drag him to a telephone booth.

"Darling," I would mumble into the mouthpiece.

Seriously.

Each evening on my return from Beata's, he would sniff my hands with pleasure - and wag his tail.

"Shove off!" I would say, pushing him away.

In the bath last night, I came up with a new expression for the dictionary of love in the computer age: *gorgeous unformatted hands*.

The evenings in Beata's attic proved insufficient (particularly in view of the fact that Agata's possible incursions were a permanent danger, and Mrs Kralova was starting to be as dangerously suspicious as the sales assistants at Kotva).

However, the school holidays were not yet over, and my wife was already back at work.

"I've got forty minutes," I would gasp into the phone, when my daughter popped out to see a friend. "Possibly fifty."

She would gulp audibly.

"Walk down to the Strakonice road," she would say. "I'll be there in four minutes."

She would arrive in what she was wearing when I called her - a dressing gown, her father's work shirt, or a T-shirt over her naked body. We would speed at about ninety miles an hour to the nearest turn-off; just before it, she would slam on the brakes and force herself into the righthand lane, horn blaring. It was only about half a mile from there to *our* forest path.

The only people I felt truly deep animosity towards that summer were *cep* gatherers.

Someone like Ed McBain, a lot of whose works our publishing house is putting out at present, would most likely have written: *In the same car and on the same highway where that summer she drove for love, a year later - just a little faster - she drove to her death.*

The heartbeats of a lover dead.

5. "So how's our *course* going?" Kral asked me one evening sometime in the middle of August. "What's the position?"

It sounded odd. Moreover, I had learnt from Petrik that he was having trouble with his business, so I had to be very careful about what I said.

"Things have greatly improved, I'd say," I replied. "Including our relationship, surprisingly enough."

"I've noticed."

I said nothing.

He observed me through half-closed eyes.

"What about her writing, then?"

It had been a long time since we had spoken about her *writing*.

"She's making a start... What I've read so far isn't half bad."

"*Making a start*?"

He scowled unpleasantly.

"I've been paying you since the end of June and *she's making a start*?"

I shrugged:

"What did you expect? That she'd be writing like Sarraut by July?"

To have used a name he didn't know was an obvious mistake:

"Can I read what she's written?" he attacked directly.

I hesitated - apart from the "Daddy and I" story (which was out of the question of course), Beata had not given me anything else of hers to read.

"Not yet."

"Why not?" he said, raising his voice.

"Denis," I said in a conciliatory tone, "what game are we playing?"

But he had hardened his heart.

"No kind of game at all," he snapped in irritation. "I just want to know what exactly I've been shoving money into these past three months."

"You feel it's been a waste of money, then?"

He wasn't going to let anything past him:

"That's exactly what I'm trying to discover!"

"Denis," I said, "try and recall: when I first came here, that dismal cave upstairs was inhabited by a mute cave newt. Go and take a look up there now."

I left a dramatic pause.

"Isn't that a *result* of some kind?" I said with conviction.

He shook his head in disagreement.

"I'm not saying that it is exclusively thanks to me - most likely she would have got over it anyway. But I've not exactly been ma-lingering, have I? Or do you think I have?"

He remained grimly silent.

"No *real* creative writing course ever took place, of course," I admitted. "But then we both know that. After all, I've never claimed otherwise... To tell you the truth, I don't know if there ever will be one."

Precisely, his reproachful expression said.

"So if you were paying me for *that kind* of course, then you're right, it would be a rather risky investment."

I sought, by using a conditional clause, to remind him that our erstwhile *contract* had undergone a rather crucial amendment al-most at the outset, namely, that I should make her *happy*.

The trouble was he didn't remember.

"A *very* risky investment," he said heatedly, but he didn't man-age to conceal a certain satisfaction that I had got myself just where he wanted me.

So that's how they do it, I thought to myself a trifle bitterly.

"I'll pay you till the end of August," he said bountifully.

He took out of his pocket the bank notes he had ready for me.

Only at that moment did the penny drop: he's *giving me the boot*.

So I really won't be here tomorrow? I realised in horror. In this beautiful kitchen? In his beautiful office? In that beautiful *Wendy* bed?

"So I'm not to come tomorrow?" I said in strangled tones.

"No," he said tersely. He looked me straight in the eye: "You can say goodbye to her today."

Everything was happening too fast.

"I don't want any more *slip-ups*, savvy?"

Quite.

"*Sir*," he said pointedly.

Zap!

So teachers don't have sex any more!

On my way up to the attic my anger rapidly grew. They suck you dry and then just spit you out! And the unions don't do a thing, of course!

While I was relating it excitedly to her, Beata gradually got undressed.

"Come here," she said at last. "Come and revenge yourself on the daughter of that disgusting capitalist..."

That was no love-making - that was a *popular uprising*.

"What are we going to do?" she said afterwards. "Where are we going to meet each other?"

"The Strakonice road."

She took it seriously.

"And what about the winter?"

I shrugged helplessly.

"How about knocking shops?" she speculated diligently.

"I know only one," I said. "And it belongs to your dad."

It was I who came up with the crazy idea, of course.

Once I'd said it - there was no unsaying it.

To tell the truth I wouldn't have wanted to.

I wanted to be with her.

And *après nous le déluge*.

"Hey," ran the crucial sentence, "come and teach at our school, then..."

IX

1. Shortly after eight o'clock on the last Monday in August, when I stepped into our office, my colleagues - with the exception of Mrs Chvatalova-Sukova, who was frantically searching for something in the drawers - were already sitting over the summer snapshots, drinking their first coffee of the 1992-93 school year.

I received a cheerful welcome.

Our traditional post-vacation reports were shortly interrupted by Chvatalova:

"Libuska," she started to whine, "you haven't seen my *triangle* anywhere, have you?"

Libuska regretted that she hadn't seen her musical triangle anywhere.

Jaromir, Lenka and Irenka hadn't seen it either.

Chvatalova-Sukova gave me a look which plainly stated who, in her view, was the main suspect in the *case of the lost triangle*.

Irenka, who had meanwhile popped over to the staff meeting room, returned with the news that a new English teacher had just joined the staff.

"So what?" said Chvatalova. "Everyone knows English."

"Where would he get hold of English teachers?" Lenka wondered. "They'd have to be supplied as *dealer's commission...*"

"He'd have to win one in *Stake and Win*," said Lenka.

I laughed along with the rest but felt a mild sense of superiority difficult to describe.

In the end I succumbed.

Their surprise was truly of major proportions.

"Beata Kralova?" Irenka repeated with unfeigned astonishment.

The repetition of that name transformed my superiority into a hot-air balloon soaring above the heads of my colleagues.

I looked down on them from on high almost with derision.

A fat lot you know about it, you poor devils! I thought to myself.

Just before nine o'clock we took ourselves off to the staff meeting room for the beginning-of-term briefing. The tables were almost all occupied already, so it was not exactly easy to save a place for Beata. At last she appeared in the doorway, dressed in a formal costume that betrayed a charming excess of zeal. She looked about her hesitantly - I waved to her. The sight of a free place brought an expression of relief, and she immediately made a bee-line for me. I enjoyed seeing how many of my male and female colleagues turned to look at us. The merry hubbub immediately gave way to a discreet murmur.

"Je-sus," she whispered.

Her eyes didn't stray from the pattern on the tablecloth.

I nonchalantly drew my chair closer to the table and placed my hand on her bare knee. She went rigid and her eyes filled with genuine terror.

She blinked in alarm.

"Relax," I said, "*Miss Kralova.*"

One of the Vice-Principals, Mrs Konopna, called the roll. Excuses were received from colleague Stribrny, in whom, according to his GP, the imminent start of the new school year had brought on *manic-depressive anxiety states*, and from colleague Steve, in whom the beginning of term had brought on a yearning to spend three more weeks in Mexico.

"Three cheers," I commented.

Our new Czech - and chiefly English - teacher, who would also be standing in temporarily for Steve, was introduced in the person of Beata Kralova.

She stood up.

I took advantage of the fact that all eyes were legitimately on her to take a good look at her myself. I couldn't help remarking to myself that our new colleague was truly good-looking. Colleague Kilian actually whistled appreciatively (he never had any difficulty audibly expressing *admiration*, though it would have been rather more chancy had he felt the need to express public *disagreement*).

Now she was one of us.

In the opening words of his beginning-of-term speech, the Principal voiced the hope that the summer holidays had filled us with sufficient new energy to be able to concentrate fully on all the challenging *educational and academic tasks* that were facing us this year, particularly - as emerged from the rest - *the re-lining of the chimneys, the construction of the much-needed third greenhouse* and the *structural modifications required on account of nutria raising.* In this connection Vice-Principal Konopna reminded us that we mustn't neglect our own teaching work.

"It looks as if we'll still have to teach this year," I whispered to Beata. "And I was looking forward to just growing cabbages."

She edged away from me disapprovingly.

The Vice-Principal then read out the class teachers for the different classes and who was sharing which office.

"Tauferova, Trakarova, Kralova," she read out among others.

Heaven help us, I thought to myself.

Curiosity forced her to lean over to me again:

"Who's Trakarova?"

I laughed.

Vice-Principal Prochazkova reprimanded me publicly and declared that a school without discipline was like a mill without water. She went on to appeal for punctual arrival at classes and for the routine practice of *pedagogical surveillance* in the corridors and over the pupils' hanging up of bags on hooks. She also drew attention to that recurrent malpractice over the years: the shifting of school desks from their marked positions, the logical consequence of which is that the desks move out of alignment and the classrooms start to look like *I'd rather not say what.* She then moved to the last item on the agenda, which was *discussion*.

The first to ask for the floor in the discussion was colleague Chvatalova-Sukova. After looking pointedly in my direction she announced *the theft of a triangle*, while expressing her amazement that there should be someone in our midst who was capable of *raising a hand against a harmless musical instrument*. She then appealed to all pedagogues present not to neglect in their teaching *the development of the emotional component of our pupils*, and expressed the view that the best medium for developing the emotional component was *beautiful music*, and best of all the music which pupils were able to hear at the well-loved *educational concerts*.

"Music," she declared verbatim, "is the food of love."

Her comments met with little understanding, however.

"Even on the shortest route," said colleague Netejkal prudently, "the return journey to the educational concert requires four public transport tickets. That makes a total of *sixteen crowns*. Sixteen crowns, that's virtually the price of - "

" - a large rum," said someone from the floor.

" - two pounds of the oranges we buy for our Risa," Vladimir continued unflappably. He was clearly reaching the nub of his argument. I was rather looking forward to it.

"I am known to most of the people here, and they would most likely agree that I'm no *trouble-maker*," he said mildly, which the people in question readily endorsed in cheerful anticipation. "Nonetheless, I wish it to be made known that I do not intend to give a fart about developing the emotional component of our pupils until such time as the school board finally pays for our tickets."

He earned the grateful applause of part of the staff and a *strong reprimand* from the administration.

Colleague Trakarova took advantage of his resentful silence to draw attention to the steady rise in the incidence of venereal diseases and tabled for consideration the question as to whether we should at last install a condom vending machine at the entrance to the dressing rooms.

"Who's that?" whispered Beata.

"Trakarova," I said.

The equivocal silence that descended on the gathering in the wake of colleague Trakarova's contribution was surprisingly broken by Jaromir, who proposed widening the scope of her plan - seeing that we will be carrying out structural modifications - and cutting out a window in the wall of the girls' dressing room. A two-way mirror could then be installed in it, which would have the twofold effect of raising the sexual awareness of passers-by and being a good money-raiser for the school.

I failed to get many colleagues to join in the applause.

The Vice-Principal stated that she failed to see why we insisted on showing ourselves to our new young colleague in the worst possible light and that the inspection of notice boards would take place that Friday.

She then dismissed us.

School is not an institution, school is an event. Petr Pitha.

After the meeting, Trakarova and Tauferova escorted our new colleague to their office. I set off for my classroom, where, resignedly, though still with a certain degree of altruism, I pinned to the empty notice board several photographs of Vitezslav Halek, Vladislav Vancura and Karel Michal and covers of their books, after which I appended the rather wilfully scribbled sentence *THEY LIVED IN ZBRASLAV...* I thereby fulfilled to the letter all the tasks required for the so-called *preparatory week* so that I could spend until Friday drinking coffee with my colleagues, chatting about the summer holidays and looking for the triangle.

That particular Monday I endured it until about eleven o'clock. Then I found some excuse to slip out of our office and jog through the maze of corridors to the other building where the classroom assigned to Beata was located. As I expected, *her* notice board still lay on a bench - over which she was fully stretched, endeavouring to push one of the many thumbtacks into the tough softboard. She had flung the jacket of her outfit onto a chair and rolled up the sleeves of her blouse. As soon as she caught sight of me, she quickly covered up the unfinished notice board with a sheet of blue crepe paper.

"I've come to give you a hand," I said.

She panted warily.

I looked around me: the green magnetic board was already covered with coloured pictures with Anglo-Czech captions, and the

132

teacher's notebook that lay on the neighbouring bench was already full of names neatly copied out. I myself was very familiar with that sort of beginner's enthusiasm, which is why I was a trifle concerned how long it would last.

"May I take a look?" I teased her.

"No!"

She was now gripping the crepe paper desperately with both hands. The stress in her arms tautened her breasts.

"*Autumn on its Way*?" I surmised. "Or *School Beckons*, perhaps?"

I touched the paper. She gripped my wrist. I noticed there was a speck of dried blood under the nail of her forefinger.

I drew it to my lips.

Her tension subsided, but she kept her eyes closed.

She removed her left hand from the paper - I uncovered the board: wild strawberries and a basket of *forest mushrooms*, beaches and yachts, temples and minarets.

"Jeepers creepers," I laughed. "*Holiday Memories*..."

"You wouldn't be needing a hand, would you?" colleague Tauferova asked from behind us.

The colour of her lipstick lent her the appearance of the *Wicked Queen*.

2. "She's *teaching* at your place?"

My wife looked genuinely surprised. Taken unawares, in fact.

"But that's just what I've been telling you..."

It took her several moments of silence to analyse my news.

"By the way: whose idea was it?"

"Mine," I said boldly.

"*Yours*?"

"What's up? I just thought it would do her good if she didn't have the time to think only about herself."

"That's true," said my wife with a certain fervour. She herself had to spend an average of fifty hours at work each week.

"You know the adage," I said. "If you want to save yourself, try and save someone else..."

"Hm," my wife said sceptically.

A couple of days later she came and sat down opposite me in the kitchen.

I laid the *Literary News* aside.

"OK - as part of your *therapeutic program* she's teaching at your place."

I nodded and waited in suspense.

"Is it also part of your therapy that she is required to come to your office for morning coffee?"

The Zbraslav information network. A dead certainty.

"I detect a hint of jealousy in your question."

"And I detect a touch of evasiveness in your answer."

Never, never, ever own up. Dr Plzak.

"I admit that she comes to our office for morning coffee and cake," I said, "but I swear I've never given her so much as a nibble!"

She didn't even grin.

"She has an office of her own - with Trakarova and Tauferova. Why doesn't she take her nibble there?"

"I couldn't say. It could be that she doesn't enjoy talk about *metastases* and *vaginal secretions* while she's eating."

"What are *metastases*?" our daughter wanted to know.

I hadn't noticed her come in.

"There's nothing else you'd like to know?" I roared in a feigned attempt at intimidation. "Don't tell me you already know what vaginal secretions are!"

"Of course I do," my daughter said. "I read about them in *Bravo*."

My wife finally laughed.

I'd got away with it that time.

Not counting the main break and occasional encounters in the canteen, the only times we met in school were when moving between our classrooms and offices. Both of us strove to leave *immediately* after the bell, which earned us ironic comments from colleagues on more than one occasion, but on the other hand we were able to guess with a fairly high degree of precision in what part of the corridor or staircase we would meet. During the first weeks of Beata's employment at the school, these were truly joyful and blessed encounters, even if we mostly dared do no more than touch fingertips or brush past each other. From time to time, however, I would be seized by a blind, ruthless courage: on those occasions, I would step in front of Beata at the last moment so that she couldn't help falling into my arms - she would resist me in panic, whimpering softly and pushing me away with her tape recorder.

The first weekends in September were particularly intolerable. On Fridays she taught an hour longer, so if I wanted to say goodbye to her, I had to interrupt her lesson.

"Remain seated, children," I would say to the fifth-year class, "I'm just bringing your teacher an urgent dispatch from the Ministry."

The children would make faces.

Each time, magnificently red in the face, she would quickly hustle me out again.

The maidenly blush. No more effective aphrodisiac.

"Shut the door," I would whisper.

She would shake her head and look about her fearfully.

I would shut it myself.

Mr Inspector, Sir.

Things weren't much better when the weekends were over. If I happened to be free, she would be teaching. And vice versa. But most importantly, every day my daughter would be waiting for me in front of the upper school.

During the whole of that September we took the Strakonice road only once.

"I was meaning to ask you something - but now I've forgotten what it was," Beata would sometimes say with plaintive irony. "Oh, yes, now I remember: Are we still going out together?"

It was straight out of Woody Allen, but it wasn't very funny.

In addition I have several other mental pictures from our shared teaching past.

First, an actual *snapshot* - a group photograph of the teachers (on account of the generous commission paid by the photographic agencies, school photographs take place at least twice a year). As directed by the photographer, the entire teaching staff tried to squeeze onto gym benches carried to the front of the school. In the background soothing verdure. In front of us, pupils screaming and making faces at us from the school windows. We pretend not to notice their taunts. Comments about breaking the lens. Perplexity in Beata's gaze: *Apart or next to each other?* Both are conspicuous. I come and stand alongside her with a smile. The movement of the row pushes us together.

Cheese.

We both look awful.

Another scene: A warm September afternoon. Indian summer. Beata and I on the benches in the avenue of cherry trees beneath Havlin. We are substituting for a work experience period. Our classes are grateful - it beats dusting the banisters. A rare, uncustomary tranquillity. No one is shouting, and the boys are not even climbing the trees. A children's roundabout creaks softly in the adjacent playground. The children are sitting or lying in the grass around us. They chew blades of grass or chat - among themselves and with us. Beata takes off her sweater, leaving on just her black sleeveless top. There is heat in the sun. The Garden of Remembrance is just a few yards uphill from us.

"Failing Poets' Corner, I'll be happy to lie here," I tell Beata. "It's lovely here. I can't stand all those morbid city crematoria..."

"We're agreed on that, then," she said.

She squints at the sun.

No one suspects anything.

The Garden of Remembrance was designed by a Zbraslav architect, Hynek Svoboda. Statues borrowed from the collections of the National Gallery fittingly complement the park's lay-out. It is an example to experts at home and abroad. Zbraslav, a special publication.

3. I already knew that Beata was incapable of doing things by halves, but even so, I was amazed to find what a good teacher she immediately became.

She did all the correct, crazy things that young novice teachers always do. She touchingly made thorough preparations, making by hand all sorts of ingenious teaching aids, and typing out and copying the texts of English songs. She played ping-pong with the kids, took them to the cinema and travelled to various sporting championships to support them (whenever I could I would travel with them, but for the life of me I was incapable of transforming myself into a frantically jubilant fan the way she did after every goal or basket scored.) She read Pestalozzi, Diesterweg and Helus. When she read somewhere about the meetings with students that President Masaryk used to hold, the very next Sunday she invited twenty-eight of her pupils to a little afternoon party. When she read some study about exercise deprivation among children, her lessons were instantly transformed into an aerobics course conducted in English. When in one of Professor Matejcka's lectures that I had lent to her she read that today's children lack respect for work - among other reasons because they have no opportunity to see their parents working - she started to take them on excursions to workplaces: *Aha, so you tilt that vibrating sieve with that lever like that and tip the dried chamomile out onto that conveyor belt? Would you mind demonstrating that once more to your Vasek and the other children, Mr Novotny?*

I lent her *Blackboard Jungle* and *Up the Down Staircase*, in order to prepare her slightly for the disappointment and disillusion that must inevitably follow in the wake of that initial euphoria, and by alluding to the countless setbacks of the protagonists of both books, I tried to convince her that a certain measure of pedagogical scepticism as well as a certain sense of futility were vital components of the professional make-up of all the best teachers - but my efforts were all in vain.

There was nothing for it. She had to experience it herself.

4. Happily she did not lose all her illusions at once - only gradually, by weekly stages, as it were.

"I don't get it," she told us, for instance, one day at break-time, "I had been over it with them *three times* - and they still didn't know a single word!"

"Why must I tidy the classroom to prepare for the cleaner?" she asked astoundedly on another occasion.

"Do I look rumpled to you?" she asked subsequently. "So why does the Principal keep trying to sell me a steam iron?"

Her questions betrayed an endearing ignorance of the workings of Czech education.

"Why do I have to sign a book to say I've signed the class register?"

There was already a note of militancy in her voice.

"Why do my kids have to sing in the choir, when they don't want to?" she asked Chvatalova-Sukova one day.

It came like a bolt out of the blue. The silence in the office was disturbed only by occasional noises from the corridor.

"I beg your pardon?"

Chvatalova looked quite appalled.

Beata repeated her question.

The coldly mocking eyes of a blinkered old lady:

"Little girl, do you know how many years I have been in the profession?"

Seventy, I surmised.

"I don't see what your length of service has to do with it!" Beata said calmly. "I'm asking you why the boys in my class have to sing when they obviously don't want to."

"Which boys? I'd like to know *which* ones."

Beata hesitated for the first time. She shot me a brief glance - I shook my head very slightly. To name was to denounce.

"You stay out of it!" she screamed at me. "You only know how to destroy!"

I'd had the same quarrel with Chvatalova-Sukova the previous year.

"Look here," I said on that occasion to the incriminated boys in my class, "do you enjoy singing?"

They sensed a trap.

"Yeah, mostly - but not in the choir."

"You don't want to go to choir?"

"No."

"No problem," I said. "Don't go, then."

The following day, as immediate retaliation for that *unheard-of rebellion*, Chvatalova-Sukova gave my whole class a test on the life of Leos Janacek. The results were worthy of inclusion in the Guinness Book of Records: twenty-three D's and failures. When she bumped into me on the corridor an hour later, she was laughing like the *Cunning Little Vixen*. I lodged an appeal with the Principal (I now find it hard to explain my naïvety at the time), from whom I obtained a half-hearted, grudging promise to *remedy the situation*. He immediately forgot about the matter for good, however, as he had to go and sign for the microwave ovens that had just been delivered.

5. I read Matejcka again yesterday. *Fighting for understanding*, I reminded myself.

And another quotation: *The only matter at issue here is how to resurrect people's ordinary interest in mutual understanding.* (Ondrej Hausenblas, "Can we make Czech lessons meaningful again?") In this connection it strikes me: Did I try to *understand* her that September?

No way. That September I tried to *sleep* with her.

I made it once.

And only once did we return to her story.

"That *silly little yarn*?" she said scornfully.

So why did she choose that one in particular? To explain her initial contemptuous behaviour, she said. Her story illustrated well her attitude to *strangers*, but it no longer had any other value for her. At the present time, she alleged, she was interested only in destroying the traditional narrative form.

"Whereas all I want to know is how to return to it," I said.

In fact, though, nothing about writing interested her at that moment; her only real ambition - it seemed to me - was to become the best teacher in Prague 5.

And now *my* ambition:

To use sensationalist journalistic means to exploit the tragic story of a twenty-year-old girl.

Consciously to calculate with the effect on readers of *kitsch vicarious experience* (Jan Lopatka).

To try and prove that contemporary literature does not only have to be, for heaven's sake, *about how hard it is to write literature* (John Fowles).

To demonstrate my erudition.

To appease my exhibitionist tendencies.

To hurt my wife.

To hurt some of my former colleagues.

To cause a scandal.

To drum up another attack on the Minister of Education.

To win another literary prize.

To make some more money.

To dispel my qualms of conscience.

To write a good novel.

(Delete where not applicable.)

My ambition... When I read that over today, it only came home to me properly for the first time that what I have been doing in this novel is to stretch *that titillating abomination: the writer's introduction* (Salinger) in order to fill a whole book.

6. At first it looked as if the fiftieth-birthday celebration for school caretaker Nedelnicek was going to be a run-of-the-mill party like countless others before in the school. Frantisek turned up with his beard smartly trimmed and in place of his almost mandatory overalls he was wearing an elegant dark suit (the one he wore on Sundays below Havlin Hill when scattering the ashes of the departed to the four winds), but the teachers straggled into the staff room very late as usual, and long after the official opening were still standing over the plates of sandwiches talking shop, which understandably did little to promote a party atmosphere.

"Happy Birthday to you!" we dutifully chorused when the gifts were presented and Beata, in whom I had confided my linguistic hang-ups, ironically offered to translate the words for me.

However, following the departure of the purely formal well-wishers and thanks to the exceptionally good wine that Frantisek had obtained in copious quantities for his jubilee celebration, the atmosphere unexpectedly mellowed. The faces of the female colleagues darkened in typical fashion and their gestures softened. Shortly, even a guitar joined in, and Jaromir began to gesticulate ever more frequently during well-known choruses. In the end he commandeered the instrument himself in order to play with his short, swollen fingers the traditional passionate protest song, *In his office he does sit, Like a fly on a lump of...coal.* At that point those members of the school administration present left in protest, contemplating aloud certain specific amendments to personal assessment ratings.

Beata looked slightly horrified.

"You're not drinking at all," I said suggestively.

The ensuing ideological anarchy meant that even the most timid members of the staff happily recalled that paradoxical tonic: singing the songs of the bad old days such as *Katyusha*, the lyrical *Song of the Plains* and the vigorous chorale *Higher and higher and higher, our emblem the Soviet star!* Meanwhile our PE colleagues had taken advantage of the noisy revelry to sneak out to their equipment store - and they returned totally kitted out for winter: Jiri Kilian had wooden cross country skis on his feet and was gripping in each hand a bamboo pole which towered several inches above him, while on his head he wore a fetching little orange bobble-hat. Helena Andelova wore a volleyball outfit and ice skates, whose rubber protectors left grey marks on the linoleum. In a bid to surpass their outstanding display, Vladimir Netejkal and Svetlana Trakarova announced a contest to see who would be the fastest at fitting a condom on a Coca-Cola bottle.

"It's an effective way of breaking down psychological barriers!" Trakarova exclaimed. She was the first to compete and achieved an extremely creditable time of six seconds.

I noticed that Beata's laughter was not altogether effortless.

"What's up?" I asked.

She shook her head.

I was surprised, I said, that someone as non-conformist as she undoubtedly was could let herself be taken in by the hypocritical bourgeois notion of the *irreproachability of teachers*, which in any case only resulted in what James Hilton in his novel *Goodbye, Mr Chips* called *the furtive, dry mustiness of old schoolmasters*.

"Hath not a teacher eyes? Hath not a teacher hands, organs, dimensions, senses, affections, passions?" I continued fervently: "If you prick him, doth he not bleed? If you tickle him, doth he not laugh? If you poison him, doth he not die?"

"All right, then," she said. "Pour me a drink."

When working on the first draft of this novel, I recalled the subsequent shenanigans and naturally conjured up scenes that would appeal to readers, such as the midnight announcement over the school PA system (with fairly convincing imitations of speeches by the Principal and the Minister), colleague Trakarova's instruction on the use of *a vacuum pump*, or two teachers making love on the floor of one of the darkened classrooms (Gentlemen, have you ever been wiped over gently afterwards with a blackboard eraser?), but all those jolly scenes are still overshadowed in my mind by one single image:

An hour or two after midnight.

Sodden serviettes and sandwich crumbs trampled into the linoleum.

The flickering flames of a number of candles.

Europe 2's late night hits.

Beata - pale from exhaustion and the wine she has drunk - dances with Frantisek Nedelnicek.

Beata in the arms of death.

A veritable tableau from Harlequin.

A story has been thought through to the end if it contains a turn for the worse. Dürrenmatt.

The connections within the plot, which the more attentive reader will have noticed here and there, are not the result of any compositional mastery but simply the logical outcome of the story's small-town setting - everyone knows everyone else, everything is bound up together.

Just to give one example: The street Za Opusem, where I still live, lies on the very outskirts of town. The scrap-metal yard, where Beata's wrecked car still stands, is situated opposite the end of the street. (That can easily be checked.)

The entire front of the car has been crushed into the driver's seat. The rear section, on the other hand, is almost unharmed apart from deep scratches in the back doors caused by the disengaging tongs. (In the face of this real death, I realised I artificially beautified the fictitious death of the young teacher in *Views on a Murder*: the tanned, *untouched* body, showing through the shallow stream of water, the *uncrushed* ribcage...)

Whenever my wife and I drive past it, I usually look away.

7. *Two essential emotions characterise the Central European mentality: melancholy and exaggerated hilarity. The one is scarcely conceivable without the other. Melancholy engenders farce, farce leaves a residue of melancholy.* Josef Kroutvor

The successful party was not without repercussions. Beata was not at school by eight o'clock, but Jaromir and I managed to arrange her teaching to be covered so that only the handful of people in the know were aware of it. At half past nine I caught sight of her from my classroom window: she was clearly feeling ill but was nonetheless *running*. I swiftly gave the children some work to get on with and dashed out to meet her. I proudly informed her that we had arranged for people to stand in for her.

"But what about my five other periods?" she gasped. "There's no way I'll make it through the day..."

"Breathe deeply," I said. "And don't talk too much, too much oxygen is fatal."

I bundled her into the pupils' cloakroom, where we waited until the bell. Then I quickly ushered her through the crowded corridors to our office.

"Oh, dear," said Lenka in a professional tone as soon as she spotted her.

"What's the matter with her?" said Chvatalova-Sukova suspiciously. "It's not infectious, I hope."

"She's feeling very ill," I said. "She put on the *Lachian Dances* by mistake."

Beata's next period was composition with the sixth-years.

"I'll collapse in the classroom," she said with concern. "Later perhaps, but not now."

She really did look bad.

"Take them up to Havlin," I suggested. "*Description of nature.*"

"I'd never manage the climb."

"What about the Castle Park, then?" said Jaromir. "That's on the level."

"What reason shall I give?"

"Statues," said Jaromir. "*Description of a work of art.* You can spend the whole hour sitting on a bench and staring at Myslbek."

I was waiting for her in front of the school when they returned. She was white as a sheet.

"How did it go?" I asked with concern.

She let the children go on ahead.

"I almost threw up over Gutfreund," she whispered wretchedly.

144

Unhappily, even my next piece of advice - that for her next period she should use the textbook *Can We Spell It Right?* (fifteen copies of which I willingly lent her from our office) was as little help to her as Jaromir's had been. The book had been published in 1983, and she unfortunately failed to notice that the exercise which she gave the children contained, among other things, several *members of the Central Committee of the Communist Party of Czechoslovakia*, one *rally of the People's Militia* and one *Soviet ice-breaker Krasin.*

However, it did not escape the attention of one of the mothers, who brought her *indoctrinated son's* writing book along to the very next meeting of the School Committee.

And the gaffe was blown.

Our pupils' pro-Western stance had been seriously jeopardised.

After fifty minutes in the Principal's office, that *crypto-communist* was no longer able to hold back her tears.

Six months loss of bonuses and merit awards - an exemplary penalty from a principal who had marched past the platform of the Central Committee of the Communist Party of Czechoslovakia on May Day marches for more than twenty years.

I wrote an article for the local newspaper.

The *Czech Daily* put one of its best journalists on the case - a twenty-year-old student from the natural history faculty.

Hey ho.

The very first thing that the school inspector for Prague 5, Dr Jiri Vagenknecht, did at our school was to sit in on a class given by the alleged instigator of all those *rebellions*: I recall how, without fear or blemish, I said something about Hrabal (while concealing, naturally, my weakness for Skala's collection *I Greet You, Windows*). It struck me, however, that the inspector genuinely wanted to get to the root of the matter, so on the way back from that period I briefly acquainted him with our successes on the path to economic independence, which, along with the pupils, we had been trying to achieve particularly by the sale of root vegetables on the main square in Zbraslav and the sale of lottery tickets in the town's various eating establishments. I went on to inform him how many greenhouses we had, how many teachers had left the school, how many of the remainder had diplomas, how long the teachers' meetings took on average, and how many D's and failures a woman teacher was capable of handing out in the course of a single lesson. And naturally I set out for him my version of the *case of the Soviet ice-breaker*, drawing his attention, for reasons of objectivity, to possible bias, dating back as far as the summer before last when the Principal labelled my theatrical skit *The Trip to Europe or Schwanda 1990* - which I also put on with the kids - *a covert attack on Prime Minister Klaus's economic reform*.

Inspector Vagenknecht listened to me attentively and made occasional notes.

He then asked me for a copy of my novel *Those Wonderful Rotten Years* which had just come out that week.

The following day he brought me in exchange Karel Siktanc's poetry collection *The Czech Astronomical Clock* (though I genuinely don't understand why that particular one).

In his report on the *in-depth inspection* he qualified all the alleged problems as being *essentially conflicts of a personal nature*.

I have sincere respect for the poet Karel Siktanc.

8. That ideological pseudo-problem was not the only repercussion which the school caretaker's successful fiftieth birthday party had - alas. The very same day that Beata was grappling with nausea someone phoned my wife at work and informed her that her husband was having a regular affair with Miss Kralova.

I repeatedly assured her that my relationship with Beata was solely one of *friendship* (which, in view of the number of our outings to the Strakonice road, was almost true), and I appealed to her not to let herself be manipulated by the malice, hatred and envy of our neighbours. However, it had no detectable effect on the size of her tears.

146

According to a poll carried out by the *Washington Post*, 97% of Americans think their spouse usually tells the truth.

I doubled my previous security arrangements, which virtually meant separation.

Beata and I went for nine days without a kiss.

We would meet in the bend of the corridor like strangers.

The action of putting my arm round Beata's shoulders required thorough conspiratorial preparations beforehand.

On the tenth day I caught sight of Beata locking the gym. I pushed her before me into the darkness of the equipment store, where beyond seven horse-hair mattresses and seven benches I tumbled her onto the trampoline in my passion.

That was the first time she pushed me away.

She spoke at great length.

Among other things she told me I was colourless.

She even criticised *our* wine bar in Horni Pocernice.

The next day the anonymous caller rang again. She gave my wife the additional information that we were now going to the PE equipment store *to screw*.

I again verified that a suitably chosen detail greatly enhances the credibility of a story.

On account of jealousy on the one hand and anger on the other, my wife and I once more failed to hear our daughter come in.

She had apparently heard plenty.

I spent the rest of the evening in her bedroom.

If you want to hear an angel cry, tell a nine-year-old girl that her Daddy is *screwing with someone else*.

That discreet wine bar in Horni Pocernice began to strike me as risky. The headwaiter looked like an informer.

My early morning erotic fantasies (which, in view of the situation, naturally increased) were no longer set in Slapy or Beata's attic, but in an out-of-the-way little hotel on the outskirts of Reykjavik, and the only way I was able to lend a bit of sparkle was to imagine that the airline connection with Prague had been interrupted.

I slept badly.
I got more frequent headaches than usual.
I also had constant stomach gas.
Retreat into illness.

And into writing, of course.

The episode I had experienced, which now caused me nothing but problems, became miraculously transformed at my desk into my only source of happiness. What a story! I used to say in elation. To write about Beata was not only thrilling, it was also safe. That was something that real life could never provide me with.

All the misfortunes of men derive from one single thing, which is their inability to be at ease alone in their room, I reminded myself bitterly in the words of Pascal.

Occasionally I would reflect on the Beata character in Beata's presence.

"Do you want to dismember still further the poor little half of you that I'm left with?" she raged.

"I'm writing about you," I protested.

"Write then! I'm not going to stop you!" she would say in annoyance. "I expect Czech literature would never forgive me if you didn't..."

9. The actual end of our relationship was as sudden as an unexpected end to a game of canasta: you have a hand of respectable, promising cards and have not by any means used up all your trumps; meanwhile, the game has come to an end, and it's all over.

It happened as follows: I was just standing outside our office door explaining to Beata with the help of a quotation from Jakob Wassermann what *man's time* meant (*A woman will never understand what man's time is. She gulps it like lemonade; however much you give her, she'll swallow the lot, but she herself has no time if she is going off to try on a hat*), when Steve appeared in the

148

bend of the staircase. He was tanned and smiling and wearing a brick-red poncho over his naked torso.

"Good heavens: Steve!" I gasped. "Head for the hills!"

I seized Beata by the arm and tried to pull her into the office before he saw us.

"Stop messing around!" she remonstrated. "Are we going to end up *running away* from people all the time?"

She pushed me away uncomprehendingly.

By now he had seen us. He flashed his dazzling teeth. Beata smiled also. I ran my tongue over my fillings and introduced them.

"Hi," said Steve.

· He looked pleased.

Beata said she had heard a lot about Steve and was really very glad to meet him in person at last. Then she asked with *sincere interest* how he had enjoyed Mexico. Steve said it had been *absolutely great*. Then he started to tell a story about some boats or other that they had had to guard at night. I cleared my throat and informed him that *unfortunately* we were in a hurry. Beata listened to my Zbraslav accent with a pained expression and said *she* was in no hurry at all.

Steve invited us home that evening to see a hundred and fifty slides and drink a couple of bottles of genuine tequila.

I told him I'd only come if the figures were reversed. I must have said it wrong because Steve didn't understand. Beata said something that I didn't understand. Steve laughed. I said that what I'd said before had only been a joke, of course - in fact I was *unfortunately busy* that evening. Steve said that was a pity. Beata said she'd come for sure - she told him that her evenings had become dreadfully boring lately. I asked her in Czech if she was intending to improve her personal profile after all those Soviet ice-breakers.

She didn't even grin.

The circle was closing.

"Let's call it off," she said. "There's no point any more."

She closed it.

X

1. *Ay me, how weak a thing The heart of woman is!* Shakespeare

"I would just like it to be the break-up of two civilised people," Beata requested of me in the days that followed. "Without all the usual spitefulness."

The fact was I had little experience of the *usual spitefulness*, but I did what I could.

"Hello, Beata. Hi, Steve," I greeted them in the corridor at school.

"Hello," Beata replied in friendly fashion. "Want to see my new tattoo?"

She pulled up her bright-coloured T-shirt (all those teacher's suits soon gave way to bright-coloured T-shirts, scarves, beads and ponchos) and showed me her naked tummy. Her navel provided the natural basis for a tattoo of an orchid flower from which a miniature hummingbird sucked nectar.

"It's... really very nice."

Steve - like Beata - also wrote. Consequently their interests complemented each other to a tee. In the morning they taught English, and in the afternoon they mostly went into the city. Mostly they would go to McDonald's to see friends, but they had also taken a liking to the Whale and FX cafés and the Godmother pizzeria. They would walk over to Jo's bar for Mexican food, which Beata, in her own words *had literally fallen in love with*. Sometimes they would also *drop by* at the offices of the local American publications, *Prague Post*, *Prognosis* and *Yazzyk*. They spent their evenings making love and writing.

Beata was of the opinion that present-day Prague was Paris of the Twenties for the Americans. I would see, she said, that something really great would emerge out of all that constant artistic and intellectual ferment, out of that *explosion of creativity* (it struck me that it wasn't so much an explosion of creativity as an explosion of private joy at the rate of the crown to the dollar, but I held my tongue). Steve's book was also *truly exceptional*, she maintained with conviction. It was set in turn in Prague, Amsterdam, Portland and the Mexican port Poza Rica de Hidalgo.

"Global thinking, get it?"

I nodded.

The main figure, she said, was a likeable American teacher, who with his Dutch friend, also at that time living in Prague, set off on holiday to Mexico. The Dutch friend was a historian who had spent several years trying to clear up a number of lesser known circumstances surrounding the death of William I of Orange, but in Prague he discovered that the topic no longer interested him, partly because he had Aids. The journey across Mexico was existential torment for the two young men, but when in a vegetarian restaurant they were duped into eating human flesh, they became reconciled to the human condition for the first time in their lives. The entire text was seemingly deliberately interspersed with *waves of emptiness* (a reference, according to Beata, to the Dutch people's centuries of struggle with the sea), and one could also detect in the rhythm of his text the rhythm of original musical instruments of the Mexican indians: the Aztec flute and the *sonajas* rattle.

"It sounds interesting," I said.

"This book is utterly free," Beata explained. "*Totally* unfettered."

"That's the way it should be."

Apparently she was translating it into Czech.

She assured me it was going to be a hit.

I look forward to reading it.

Only now in retrospect do I admit to a hypocritical nonchalance and a pretence at being in the know when calmly receiving from

Beata, without batting an eyelid, all those crazy, shocking pieces of news. Heaven forbid that I should betray I wasn't *in*!

"We go a lot to that American launderette in the Dejvice neighbourhood..."

"Really? That's great..."

"I don't mean to do our washing - just for the heck of it. It's a fantastically friendly place."

"So I've heard..."

Or on another occasion:

"I believe people should always fix themselves a nearer milestone..."

"Definitely."

"It doesn't matter what you call it. Simply something you have to achieve. For Steve and me it's bunji-jumping."

"Wow - you're brave..."

"Yeah, I suppose so."

(Fortunately the police banned them from doing it.)

But few understood as precisely as Capek, that going overseas, joining the army, finding buried treasure, making a pact with the Devil, killing a dragon or winning the hand of a princess were never regarded in fact as a higher degree of authenticity, but its opposite, that it all bordered on a kind of disturbance or disorder... Less and less are people truly capable of fulfilling their destiny, being themselves. So in the end all that remains is confusion and shame over events and actions whose authenticity is very questionable. Josef Jedlicka

2. At night I would sit in the dark in the dentist's chair.

To look for favourable signs, was my intention.

To re-discover humour.

For McMurphy knows you have to laugh at the things that hurt you, just to keep the world from running you plumb crazy.

But it was slow going and I slept little.

The twenty-ninth of September was my saint's day.

My daughter bought me Palmolive shaving foam:

152

"*Good morning!*" I discovered written in English under the cap next morning.

Fuck you!

Mornings with my daughter...

While I was still teaching I would prepare breakfast for the two of us. Once - before her eighth birthday - I couldn't find the yoghurts which I'd bought the previous day. Eventually I found them in the garbage pail.

"They were old," my daughter protested.

"Don't be so silly!" I snapped at her.

I looked for a date of some kind:

Troja creameries - founded 1870, I happened to notice.

My daughter. My little angel.

But why am I telling this?

She helped me a lot. Writing helped me a lot, too. Plus the crutches of my daily duties. Likewise, that dentist's chair was not over-comfortable. In other words, my reluctance to *really* suffer was a help too.

Even Agata tried to help me in her way. She took it totally for granted that she would take her elder sister's place. She started with veiled provocation: fixing me with a steady gaze, touching me with her budding breasts and stroking me like a sick rabbit. Later it apparently occurred to her that she should instead make an effort to prove to me she was no longer a little girl and would make a point of speaking to me about her *past lovers*. When she subsequently invited me to a *private party* to celebrate her fifteenth birthday (it fortunately coincided with a visit to Germany), her gaze expressed her unwavering conviction that she would make me as good a mistress as Beata.

One day I met her mother in the shopping centre - I was gratified that she came and greeted me spontaneously.

"How's your husband?" I responded.

"Doing business," she replied with contempt. "He'll die of a heart attack before two years are out."

153

There was something frightening in the matter-of-fact way she said this.

She took me gently by the hand:

"If only you knew what they've done to her room... You just can't imagine!"

I could imagine.

"That girl is insane," said Mrs Kralova. "Kral is just too frightened to admit it."

That same matter-of-factness.

"We all are a bit," I said reassuringly.

"Well OK," she objected, "but *that* insane?"

A short English-Czech glossary:
start up an engine - *spustit motor*
step on the gas - *seslapnout plyn*
let in the clutch - *pustit pedal spojky*
at top speed - *plnou rychlosti*
fly-over - *premosteni*
suicide - *sebevrazda*

We disclose reality by ridding ourselves of worn-out modes of narration. Robbe-Grillet

And just one further comment on narrative technique (which occurred to me when I was mentioning Kral): Chekhov maintained that if an author mentions a gun in a story or novel, it should actually be used to shoot with later - *i.e.*, it shouldn't be mentioned *fortuitously*. I am therefore aware of the fact that if Kral has been accompanied by two armed guards from the very start of this story without either of them actually shooting a gun, this unwritten literary law has been broken. It's regrettable, but that's the way it was. Life sometimes defies the laws of literary creation (I could, of course, have Kral bumped off by two Ukrainian mafiosi in the U Holubu restaurant in Smichov, or alternatively, arrange for him to be tied to a girder at the bottom of some dam, but something prevents me from treating a real person in that way).

154

3. Today was All Souls' Day. On the gates of the Garden of Remembrance I read a publicity leaflet from the Friends of Cremation Society:

When my heart is turned to ash
Throw it to the winds
To fade in the grass of the meadows.
Nothing much.

I laid my five roses on the rocks sloping down to the said *meadow* - I've had them since yesterday in a jam jar on the balcony. As I was leaving the house with my bouquet today, I noted the odd fact that my wife is even jealous of cremated girls scattered to the four winds.

Beata informed me that Steve had invited her to Portland for Christmas.

On Thanksgiving Day.

"I wouldn't mind a bit of turkey either," I said.

It's almost unbelievable how many American men in Prague quickly find a partner. American women are far less lucky in that respect and point disgustedly at new relationships in which, they allege, "patriarchal American men seek submissive partners". The angst-ridden feminism of American women has already succeeded in frightening away tens of thousands of men, and the runaway Americans are by no means seeking partners in Europe alone. Vera Chase, *Literary News*

A year ago, just a couple of days after All Souls' Day, Jaroslav Koran suggested I write a story for *Playboy*. At that time I had only my teacher's salary to rely on once more, so I happily accepted his lucrative offer.

"I've written a story for *Playboy*," I boasted to Beata in the school canteen.

She teasingly stared at my crotch: "What's it about, for heaven's sake?"

She merrily interpreted for Steve.

"It's about you. It's called *The Female Intellectual*."

The story was published in April of the following year.

I thought long and hard about whether to include it in this book - for one thing, it bears the marks of having been written to cater to the requirements of a specific readership, and for another, the casting of myself in the role of a *divorced playboy* must needs have a comic effect after everything I've said about my marriage so far, and thirdly, even I find that such transitions to quite a different story are generally disruptive (*e.g.*, I don't think it was a good idea for Irving to have incorporated "Garp's" stories into his excellent novel *The World According to Garp*). The fact that I finally decided in favour of its inclusion is solely because of my steadfast conviction that, in spite of outward differences, I am writing the same story (besides which I couldn't resist demonstrating my brilliant intuitive powers in prophesying Beata's subsequent *ecological* activity).

The Female Intellectual

If cruel fate or the district military board should ever decree that you are to spend eleven months in a cramped caravan with one other person and a crackly radio, then you will undoubtedly need to arm yourself with enormous patience. If, moreover, that caravan stands in middle of a deserted frontier zone and the person in question starts every morning by noisily blowing his nose into the tin handbasin and then laying into you because you got into university and he didn't, then you'll need to make considerable efforts to preserve your sanity. But if, to cap it all, you are obliged to share with that person not only the army's monthly Atom *with its single crossword but also the only daughter of a rather despotic woodcutter from a fairly distant secluded cottage, then you have no alternative but to make up your mind once and for all either to blow the head off your companion with the service weapon provided - or to make friends with him. After careful consideration of both alternatives, Oskar and I chose the second. When later the period of our joint service was drawing to a close, I couldn't help thinking to myself that whilst in future I would gladly forgo the snot in the handbasin, I might well come to miss Oskar himself and his cheerful ribald speech, not to mention his culinary speciality, forester's steak (served rare). Unhappily on the day that our paths were supposed to diverge for good, Oskar had to have a glass or two too many in the King of the Bohemian Forest restaurant, and in the unshakeable conviction that he was entering the smoking section of the local train to his native Hlinsko, boarded the express bus with me to Prague, where, in the days that followed, he settled for good.*

Things that come into being on command tend not to have much of a shelf life, but my friendship with Oskar that emanated from two sets of call-up papers turned out to be the proverbial exception to prove the rule: Oskar's old dark blue Renault was permanently parked beneath my apartment window, and for years that very car would take me on vacation, to friends' funerals and divorces. Furthermore, Oskar was later engaged as a driver by the firm where I was working and before long became my own unofficial private driver. I enjoyed going places with him because he knew a lot of great yarns and even better transport cafés, but most of all because he was not at all bound by the well-known rules of politeness governing company drivers. On the contrary, he would always return to our earthy Bohemian Forest phraseology of earlier days.

"I wouldn't mind interfering in her internal affairs," he would say on catching sight of some good-looking girl in a town we were driving through, and he would grin suggestively like he did that time when, on his return from the woodcutter's daughter, he scrubbed the purple juice of crushed bilberries off his knees in the tin handbasin.

I was mostly happy about this as it seemed to me that if we gave up entirely our national service vocabulary, we would be giving up something that was intrinsic to our friendship, which came about at a time when, in Oskar's words, foxes' holes were the only ones available *on occasion.*

But then we met Beata.

Just two minutes after I broke the rules that rainy morning and permitted him to stop for that drenched girl hitch-hiker, I was already regretting my decision. Two hours later I knew it was one of those errors rightly described as fatal.

Muddy toes in leather sandals, a long hand-sewn skirt with bits of thread sticking out all round, and an enormous black T-shirt whose sagging neckline revealed over and over again her small naked breasts. The English words on the T-shirt requested us - if I translated the nonsense correctly - "not to send girls' souls coloured postcards from trips to moors". The girl herself informed us in Czech, while removing a little knapsack obviously full of books, that her name was Beata and that she was travelling to the Sramek festival in Pisek.

"Sramek?" Oskar exclaimed delightedly.

It turned out that Oskar had once read Silver Wind *and seen* Month on the River *on TV about a year before. Despite the fact that Beata refused to comment on the film version of* Month on the River *and regarded* Silver Wind *to be* a painfully transparent fictionalisation of adolescence, *they managed to talk on the topic for a full thirty minutes. Oskar, to my amazement, even recalled the word* impressionism, *though Beata indulgently explained to him that it was no more than* a torn canvas that Sramek used to throw across the bare theses of his themes in a naïve attempt to mask them. *Oskar conceded that that might indeed be the case from a certain point of view - while his* actual *point of view was at that moment determined by the imaginary connection between his blue eyes, the rear-view mirror and Beata's decolletage. Beata declared that the only things that had more or less outlived Sramek were six or seven early poems and* The Body, *of course - that had literally fascinated her at one time, she said. And even though the novel had now* palled *on her somewhat, she was nonetheless intending* to bring it up to date as a scenic psychodrama. *After a moment's reflection, Oskar replied that it could well be a surprisingly good idea. I maintained a grim silence. Then Beata asked Oskar*

158

*if he enjoyed being a driver. Oskar protested that he was no driver
but was only thinking about what to do with his life - and driving
had always provided him with the best opportunity for thinking.
He might go off to the Alps, or he might try returning to his studies.
At the moment he was telling her this he wasn't touching the wheel
at all; he had his hands in his lap and was leaning back dreamily
against the headrest. His foot on the accelerator maintained a
constant speed of seventy-five miles an hour.*

"Keep your eyes on the road," I said.

"Don't you like Sramek's Body?" Beata assailed me.

"No," I said. "And his body definitely wouldn't get me to go to
Pisek."

*She looked at me with pity, but in reality she was feverishly try-
ing to think how best to offend me. At last she decided to pick on
my tie. She leaned over to my seat and seized it finically with her
fingertips.*

"What's this, for heaven's sake?" she asked in disbelief.

"Guess," I said calmly.

Her type is incapable of ruffling me any more.

"I'll give you three chances: either a) a common item of European male attire known as a tie; b) my prolapsed colon; or c) an
amulet to protect men from female intellectuals."

*She didn't smile this time either, but I wasn't surprised. The
only time girls like her laugh at jokes is when they come across
them in books by a little-known author, preferably English or
American. Though I don't think this one would have smiled even if
James Thurber himself were sitting next to her.*

Instead she asked spitefully:

"You've had dealings with female intellectuals, then? I'd be
amazed to know where."

"Just one," I replied modestly. I pointed at her bag: "She came
to our last divorce hearing with a knapsack just like that one."

In the end she couldn't help a brief snigger.

"You've got teeth!" I exclaimed in surprise.

She pursed her lips in disdain.

"Go ahead and show them," I said, fixing my eyes on her exposed breasts. "You've nothing to be ashamed of."

For the next fifteen minutes she held her tongue. Then she declared that she hadn't managed to have breakfast and would be glad of a coffee, too. I deliberately made no comment, but after about ten miles, Oskar turned off into a service area. I raised my eyebrows enquiringly but he didn't notice, as he was checking with uncustomary diligence the details of his driving instructions for that day.

The restaurant, which I'd not visited before, was unexpectedly cosy - vaulted ceilings, newly painted white walls, honey-coloured curtains and windows, leather-patterned floor tiles, massive oval tables, clean linen tablecloths, golden everlasting flowers in coarse earthenware vases. The menu had a yellow canvas cover. It went some way towards improving my mood.

"These new-fangled rustic creations," Beata proclaimed, after looking around her, "are going to be terrorising our senses absolutely everywhere from now on, I fear."

"A real mess...," Oskar grumbled in agreement.

The headwaiter arrived. Beata gave him the sort of look that most people reserve for possible encounters with jelly-like aliens and ordered filtered coffee with milk, plain yoghurt, two slices of toast, camembert cheese and one poached egg garnished with chives. The waiter gave a dry laugh and went to check with the kitchen. He returned shortly and his light-coloured wooden tray bore everything bar the camembert cheese - though he did offer Beata the choice of several other varieties. Beata refused each of them in turn and ordered a pineapple juice in addition. I had this unshakeable feeling that I was sitting opposite my ex-wife, and I offered the waiter a look of mute sympathy.

"If you're as servile as that with an ordinary waiter, I'd hate to see how you behave towards a traffic cop...," Beata scolded me after he'd gone.

I told her that an encounter with a traffic policeman was increasingly likely in view of the fact that Oskar's eyes had been lately fixed on her bosom and not the road - but even so I did my best not to kowtow to the guardians of the law.

During her breakfast we were treated to some of Beata's other opinions. Today's rightwing parties seemed to her slimily utilitarian whilst those on the left were vulgar and stickily populist. The political centre was a myth created by people afraid of their own opinions. Our culture was as unworthy of the name as a group of little islands in the middle of the ocean was unworthy of the name of a continent. Education was exhausted from centuries of pretending to pupils, parents and teachers that it was meaningful. She considered cork flooring to be covert snobbery. She found Hitchcock extremely amusing while for some irrational reason skating children caused her anguish. Gandhi's ideas would have appealed to her if he hadn't been so inexplicably absentminded. A woman's body was capital that men took possession of without compensation. I was essentially a dead, burnt-out individual, whereas within Oskar there was something that even he was not yet aware of.

"A tumour?" I suggested, but she did not consider me worthy of a riposte. This world's last chance was empathy she continued. It would be decided in the next six, or at most, eight years. If things turned out well, then the next century would be an age of thought transfer. After all, all things were interlinked - that vase on the table could well have some unknown cosmic message for us.

"A rustic cosmic message," I said.

Even then I knew that I was wasting my time. However ironic were my comments in my efforts to unmask her for Oskar's benefit, they were in vain. A blind man can't even see the mask, let alone the face beneath. A blind man sees nothing.

"It is necessary to fight people like you," she told me with unconcealed antipathy.

"But how?" Oskar asked fervently.

He was lost. I realised it before we got to Pisek, where she mutely passed him her telephone number with a bewitching look.

The next weeks and months only confirmed me in this conviction, unfortunately. Oskar stopped visiting me and avoided me at work. When I confronted him with it, he told me he didn't have the time as his evenings were taken up with writing an essay on the phenomenon of speed in the modern world.

161

"An essay?" I repeated, to make sure I had not misheard him. "An essay? About the phenomenon of speed?"

"Yeah," said Oskar. "Beata asked me to write it."

So there he was spending his evenings writing an essay. Some time afterwards Beata moved in with him, allegedly to give him a bit of a hand with punctuation. Oskar let his beard grow and started tying a woven scarf round his head, so he ended up looking like a younger version of Yasser Arafat. They sold Oskar's furniture and transformed his bedroom into a studio, where they tore up and chewed magazine cuttings, old posters, tram tickets, Beata's written messages and electoral registers and used the resultant material to create "private political artefacts". They smoked grass and ate sweetcorn. They adopted a stray dog, two thrushes that were supposed to have fallen from the nest, and a white rat that was confused from constant experiments in a research institute.

"It's not much better off, then," I commented.

Oskar didn't even grin. He only laughed at jokes that Beata laughed at. He only went to films she bought tickets for. He only went to exhibitions that were held in some tatty cellar or tatty passage in the Little Quarter. He'd spend his evenings at the Bunker or the Mamma Club. He told me I looked like an old fogey. He'd lost about twenty pounds and started falling asleep at the wheel. When, one afternoon on the way back from Strakonice, we drove at full speed into a field of rye, my patience was exhausted. Oskar made a feeble pretence of wanting to pick some grains to make muesli, having allegedly mistaken it for an oat field.

"Aaaahh!" I bellowed, half out of my wits, while Oskar reversed onto the road. "Aaaahh! I've had enough! Enough!"

Nothing more was said for the rest of the journey. At Zbraslav I made him turn off and drive up to the church at Havlin. I got out and angrily slammed the door. I set off in the direction of the graveyard - I knew my way as I had been a frequent visitor there during the period when my marriage was heading for divorce. Oskar followed me in mystified obedience. I couldn't even bring myself to look at him: the scarf knotted over his forehead, the crumpled cotton shirt hanging outside his trousers, the shabby moccasins, and around his neck a miniature glass bottle containing some weird liquid. Whatever's in it? I asked myself angrily. Holy water? Crocodile tears? Virgin's blood? Ladislav Klima's sperm? Jesus Christ, enough! I cursed silently.

I halted in front of Maratka's statue The Intelligentsia. How well I knew it! The hanging head, the slumped shoulders, and the haggard face with its expression of unimaginable suffering. And around the sunken eyes an eternal, never ending shadow. I grabbed Oskar by the back of his neck:

"Take a good look, you idiot," I ordered him with uncontrollable fury. "That's the way you'll end up. Just like that!"

The nape of Oskar's neck tried to escape my grip, but I tightened it all the more as I came to realise that human experience was, is and ever will be incommunicable.

"Look, this is where all her cognition leads!" I yelled into Oskar's face. "To this! To this!"

Two old ladies were coming down the path from the Garden of Remembrance. I forced Oskar onto the nearest bench and spoke to him for twenty long minutes.

"You see things too simply," Oskar eventually said wearily. "The world isn't so simple. And anyone who acts as if it is is only lying to himself."

"So lie, then!" I appealed to him. "Can't you understand that you won't cope without lies like that?"

I made one further attempt and told him about the hero of Italo Svevo's novel - how, when a lame friend explains to him how each human step is made up of fifty-seven separate movements of muscle and sinew, he himself starts to limp, too.

"Don't you understand now, for God's sake?!" I implored him.

Oskar said that he didn't know the novel in question unfortunately, because - unlike me - he didn't get into university. Then he said we ought to be going because that evening he and Beata were organising a sort of little protest happening with some reasonable anarchists.

At that moment I gave it up once and for all. I didn't even ask what they were protesting about.

About two weeks later, during one of our business trips, Oskar bought a school blackboard and easel. Having hauled them to the car, he asked me in rather formal tones whether he might be allowed to take them back with him to Prague.

"Do what you like," I said rudely.

However, he felt he had to explain to me the purpose of his rather outlandish purchase and treated me to a short lecture. He told me that one can easily get lost in the torrent of words that people use. Words, I was to understand, ebbed and flowed like the tide, and the individual is unable to hold onto them long enough to understand them. That's what causes so much misunderstanding among people. It's surprising, he said, how easily one may overcome such misunderstanding just with an ordinary blackboard and a piece of chalk.

"I see," I said in disgust. It was just so familiar. At the time when my ex-wife and I were losing ourselves in a torrent of words, we used to write each other long letters. She used a typewriter. Oddly enough she didn't think of a blackboard and chalk.

Nothing is more exhausting than useless striving. I felt I needed a vacation, and although I usually go at high season, on this occasion I took it in early July. And I didn't regret it. Even before we'd arrived in Pula, I had made the acquaintance of the young woman in the next seat. Her name was Zuzanka and she was delightfully uneducated. Fate had seemingly decided at last to pay me back some of what it owed me.

"What do you think about cork flooring?" I asked Zuzanka, for instance, just for the sake of comparison.

"It's nice and practical," she said ingenuously. "You just give it a wipe over..."

My heart sang. We didn't talk politics and I don't think she'd even heard of Gandhi. We used to go to a little open air wine restaurant right on the sea shore. The waiters wore striped T-shirts under their jackets, and from the beams there hung imitation fishing nets in which shone orange and red paper lanterns shaped like starfish and sea horses. The first time we entered it, I must admit I was a bit concerned how she would react.

"It's nice here!" Zuzanka exclaimed with apparent sincerity.

I think I really was in love with her. When, a few days later I seized the capital of her body without compensation, *she looked*

164

almost grateful. Usually I start to get a bit bored towards the end of a vacation, but I was genuinely loath to leave Pula.

I put off meeting Oskar for a whole week after my return, but in the end I couldn't bear it any longer and summoned him to my office.

"Hi. How was the vacation?" he enquired dutifully without any trace of interest. He looked even worse than ever. Apart from anything else his hands shook slightly.

"Great. The shellfish still keeps repeating on me, but otherwise great. I screwed myself silly," I replied Bohemian Forest-style.

At the mention of screwing, *Oskar visibly winced. He noticeably turned his head away.*

That marked the end of my vacation.

"What's up?" I asked with resignation.

"Nothing," Oskar said. "Things aren't too good for us in bed at the moment."

The following day we were due to go to Liberec for an arbitration case, and Oskar had originally promised to call for me at six in the morning. When he hadn't arrived by half past six, I phoned him at the car pool, but they had no news of him or the car. The foreman sounded annoyed. I wasn't surprised.

Docilely I set off for Oskar's place. The company car - which looked as if it hadn't been washed for weeks - stood in front of the house. I rang the bell three times before Oskar opened the door. Despite the fact he was dressed in some kind of Japanese pyjamas, he didn't appear to have slept much that night. He blinked his red eyes at me in surprise from beneath puffy eyelids. I was glad he actually recognised me.

"Oh, yeah - sorry," he apologised distractedly. "Come in, I'll be right with you."

The apartment looked like an anarchist secretariat. The wallpaper that we once chose together had been ripped off, and the bare walls were covered in hundreds of newspaper cuttings which were gradually coming unstuck. All that was left of the old furniture were two oak cupboards on which the rescued thrushes were crawling about and making droppings. The new additions were two writing desks and an oil barrel that served as a coffee table.

The double bed from the erstwhile bedroom had been equipped with a sky-blue canopy. And fixed to the canopy was a sign saying I'm at the post office. God.

"Jesus Christ," I breathed softly.

Oskar shrugged. The moment I'd entered, Beata had gone and locked herself in the bathroom in protest, so Oskar was obliged to shave in the bedroom: he had to crouch down to do so, as the socket was at floor level and the shaver had a short cord, and with his free hand he had to keep parrying the attentions of the white rat. The entire scene filled me with anguish, the sort of anguish Beata felt when watching children skating - and I preferred to turn my back on Oskar. In the corner in front of me I spotted the famous blackboard. On it was written: You maintain that your orgasm is conditional on my sincerity throughout the entire previous day.

The writing was fairly neurotic. Oskar wiped the blackboard abstractedly. I had a feeling he was going to collapse for good at any moment.

The car was in a similar state - apart from the bald tires and a broken headlight, the gears were playing up. I didn't dare criticise him for it; after all, if someone has anarchists and thrushes to take care of, they can hardly look after a car as well. On the fourth attempt, Oskar managed to put it into gear and we drove off. From inside the car I could hear rather unusual sounds from the engine.

"I must be impotent," Oskar said hoarsely after a while.

"Congratulations."

Oskar's eyes, fixed on the distant horizon of the road, shone damply.

"I've no sympathy for you," I said harshly. "I gave you fair warning."

I started seriously to consider changing my driver.

"What do you think about healers?" Oskar asked all of a sudden.

"Nothing," I snapped. "I don't think anything about them at all. I don't think anything about anyone or anything. Take a leaf out my book and you won't have any need for healers!"

He said nothing in reply, but just before one of the next cross-roads, he started to drive much more slowly and asked whether he might make a detour to see a healer who lived only a couple of minutes' drive from there.

"No way," I said adamantly. "We're late as it is."

Oskar pulled over to the hard shoulder and stopped.

"I'm not going anywhere!" I persisted.

Oskar switched off the engine.

"Beata says he's one of our best psychotronic practitioners," he whimpered in the ensuing silence.

"Aaaahh!" I roared in impotent despair. "Aaaahh!"

Oskar waited patiently.

"Aaaahh!" I roared liberatingly as my entire body strained against the seatbelt. I thumped the dashboard with my fists - several cigarette butts fell into my lap along with a ripped copy of Vokno *review and a tatty card giving the visiting hours at the Bohnice mental hospital.*

"I'll come and visit you every other Wednesday," I informed Oskar, after examining it more closely. "Does that suit you?"

He informed me matter-of-factly that they only went there to visit several less serious patients with whom they were trying to put on a performance of Kafka's Metamorphosis.

"If a doctor catches you, he'll kill you," I warned him.

He told me there were doctors involved too.

"Oh, I see," I said.

Oskar started the motor.

"Can I, then?"

"Go where you like, you damned fool!" I roared. "Can't you see that not even Lourdes would help you?"

From looking at the villa in which the folk healer dwelt, one could tell that its owner indeed helped many sufferers and that they in turn helped him. I refused to leave the car. The entire visit lasted no more than a quarter of an hour.

"What? Finished already?" I asked him in astonishment when Oskar was once more seated alongside me. "If it takes him only fifteen minutes to turn a man into a stud bull, then he really must be the best."

167

"He's going to treat me remotely," Oskar said with restraint. "At ten o'clock this evening."

I said nothing for a long time.

"Fine," I eventually said. "And now, my dear Oskar, would you kindly drive me to the arbitration session. I want to go to this arbitration. I don't think I've ever looked forward so much to spending a day at arbitration. Get a move on!"

The arbitration did indeed fulfil all my expectations: it was extremely tedious, long-winded and, technically speaking, largely pointless; but on the other hand, it enabled me to spend seven hours in the company of people endeavouring to put their education and experience to a life-asserting purpose instead of as a weapon against themselves. When it was over, I spent about another hour walking round the shops without having anything in particular to buy, and with rather uncharacteristic enjoyment, I chatted here and there with sales staff about imported coffee-makers, fertilising indoor plants, and the difficulties of drilling into concrete panels. I then returned to the company car a good half hour later than I'd agreed with Oskar. We drove off in deep silence - which, however, was a lot preferable, I realised, to anything Oskar and I could have said to each other. Happily I managed to fall asleep fairly soon.

When I awoke, I saw we were standing just beneath the brow of a gentle wooded slope, in some kind of small muddy clearing. To my left there were two stacks of cut timber which completely blocked off my view of the road. The last remnants of daylight could be seen between the trees on the horizon, but here in the woods it was fairly dark already. Oskar stood motionless above the open front hood: shoulders slumped, head hanging. His dark silhouette reminded me of the statue in the Garden of Remembrance.

I turned the key in the ignition, and a pleasant greenish glow lit up the dashboard. I switched the radio on quietly and leaned back comfortably against the headrest. It occurred to me that in this position and with nice quiet music in the background I was ready to face any tidings fate had in store for me - even the news of my death if need be. Still less could I be ruffled by alarming tales of

168

broken gearboxes or carburettors, and there was no way at all that I could be bothered by talk about some girl with her heart confused by too much theory. A warm wind moaned in the treetops. It reminded me of the Bohemian Forest.

The door opened. The fragrance of the woods wafted in. Oskar collapsed into the driver's seat.

"I can't take any more!" he moaned.

I couldn't tell whether he had in mind Beata or the engine, but I couldn't have cared less really. Life, blessed life, I said to myself in some sort of inexplicable euphoria.

Meanwhile it all came spilling out of Oskar. How if he switched the light off, she would ask him if he was afraid of the truth of light. How if he left the light on, she would ask sarcastically if he intended to flaunt his cosmetic flaws in a hundred-watt glow. How if he was slow, she would ask if he'd fallen asleep. How if he was impulsive, she would ridicule him for acting like a diminutive Michael Douglas - or ask whether he was haunted by the ghost of his father's penis. How if he was importunate, she would call him a selfish lecher and if he wasn't, she would call him frigid. How he was still in love with her after all. How he still found her incredibly arousing! Oskar became more and more agitated as he spoke. How was it possible that what turned him on most of all was just thinking about her? He only had to think of her tits! Those firm little tits! There was something in his voice that made me turn my gaze to him: his eyes were closed, his breath came in quick pants. His cheeks had darkened.

"Her little pussy!" he blurted. "Her sweet little mound! Her lovely pussy!"

Oskar's emaciated hips were thrusting forward to meet something invisible. His head hung lower and lower. His right hand, which until then had rested limply on the gear lever released his member from the constricting fly in a single movement. I looked slowly and thoughtfully at the clock: it was a couple of minutes past ten.

He cried out.

He slumped forward. A powerful, translucent jet shot through the half-light.

169

Shortly afterwards he started to breathe calmly.

Oskar fell asleep.

I let him sleep for half an hour before gently waking him. He had to repair the car and set off for that world that continued to defy simplified explanations.

4. In November I started to read once more. In December I wrote a score of literary parodies which I assembled into a slim volume entitled *Stand By for Take-off.*

I called the gradual hardening of my heart, *rediscovering my capacity for ironic detachment.*

In other words things started to change for the better.

I was offered an editor's job in the Czech Writers publishing house (we agreed that I would go on teaching at least until the January holiday and start there in February). Further favourable reviews of *Those Wonderful Rotten Years* appeared.

By Christmas I was all right again.

The whole family came together on the Sazava on Christmas Day. The dogs brawled noisily, the grandmothers sang carols, Grandad kept choking on fishbones, and the little three-year-old son of my screenwriter brother went round threatening to kill everyone, but it struck me that this was the calmest Christmas I had known in my whole life.

In her new knitted outfit my daughter started to move like an adolescent girl.

In my wife's beautiful eyes nothing showed at last but the reflected candlelight.

Her present to me was a Parker fountain pen.

Just so I knew my place.

When I returned to school after the New Year, I was informed that Steve would not be coming back from the States that year. Apparently Beata had not gone to America at all.

I thought about her several times during that morning, but we didn't meet even once in the corridor. After lunch I made my way to her office.

170

She was squatting Turkish fashion under the window, sipping some sort of hot carrot juice and reading Simone de Beauvoir's *Second Sex*. Had she instead been sitting at the table drinking coffee and reading the *Lidové noviny*, it would have been a bad sign, but as it was, things looked entirely in order.

"I was too *free* for his taste," she explained, using the English expression. "It seems he was shocked about me having that tattoo..."

She spoke almost cheerfully.

"You hadn't enough *Slav domesticity* in you," I said with relief.

"*To be a proper woman means being incompetent, small-minded, passive and subservient,*" she read to me. Apparently too much education or independence terrifies men. The dumb blonde supposedly always wins out over the intellectual woman. Any assertion of personality diminishes a woman's femininity. The intellectual woman admittedly knows that she ought to be a spontaneously offered object, but whenever she plays the powerless woman, she appears unconvincing.

"*A face feigning naïvety suddenly lights up with too-obvious intelligence...,*" Beata quoted to me animatedly.

"So why do you play the naïve woman?" I said a trifle absent-mindedly.

"What sort of stupid question is that? Do you ever bloody listen to me, for fuck's sake?"

She had clearly embraced *the racy cynicism of the older woman*, that well-known *outcome of frustrated anticipation*.

XI

1. January was the last month of my teaching career.

I started to carry home the works of literature I had brought to my office in the course of my time at the school. Now and then during lessons I would walk down the row of desks and observe the children's heads bent over their open writing books; I tried to discover whether I was moved, but either I was suppressing my feelings unduly or they were non-existent because I remained, though not indifferent, still self-composed. One weekend I corrected the last sixty assessment compositions, this time on the subject *A frightening experience*. At least half of the stories were about a scary journey to a dark cellar, while the requisite fright was generally caused by a jar of apricots falling off a high shelf (*the blood froze in my veins*) or by a dog called Rex who unexpectedly rubbed against the story-teller's leg (*and the shock took my breath away*).

I gave them all B's or A's.

Soon the children started going around with solemnly secretive expressions. I realised they were already collecting for my present.

"Don't you dare go spending a lot of money on some enormous fluffy toy," I warned them. "I'd sooner have a bottle of scotch..."

They exchanged bewildered looks.

"Aha," I realised, "have I gone and put my foot in it?"

They nodded reproachfully.

In the end I got both a teddy bear and a bottle of scotch.

I was so moved I invited them home.

Like Masaryk.

A short balance sheet: In the course of my almost four years of school teaching I spent nigh on one thousand hours with the children of my class. I wrote and directed two school theatrical productions. I confiscated one flick-knife, two fireworks and two pornographic playing cards. In line with my optimistic temperament I tell myself there was some purpose to it all. I experienced four ministers of education and three principals: the first of them - who was imposed - I helped to depose, the second I helped to elect. The third one was once more imposed. I attended almost one hundred meetings of different kinds: consultations, boards, committees, steering groups, founding conferences and protest rallies and wrote about two dozen discussion papers, memoranda, policy statements, petitions, newspaper articles, open letters and proposals to improve the running of the school. In spite of my optimism, I fear that it was all a waste of time.

This novel is my final *complaint*.

Beata and I agreed that we would hold a joint farewell party.

To find out how many dinners to order at the Kotva restaurant, Beata stuck up an invitation in her office asking for those interested to sign up. I was rather fearful about the response, as the very act of signing an invitation from us was tantamount to a demonstration of opposition, but the final tally of names came as a pleasant surprise - with only one or two exceptions, the only names missing were those I expected to be.

Beata chose to wear one of her former outfits. It really suited her. The guitars twanged.

I drank as if I were driving.

I noted with relief that my vigilance against any possible *backsliding* was slightly greater than Beata's.

It was only with the arrival of the champagne that the unproclaimed *friendly restraint* championships were brought to an end. We went and sat apart from our colleagues and very soon we even revived the erstwhile charm of our long-lost amorous vocabulary.

"Don't be sad, Man-child," I said. "If you like, Mowgli, I'll bring you a posy of orange-blossom."

"Thank you, Baloo," Beata said tenderly. "We be of one blood, thou and I."

She even kissed me lightly.

"As tender as a young bamboo shoot," I said with relish.

I yearned to kiss her once more, but fortunately, in the nick of time I caught sight of Jaromir bringing leftovers for his cats from the kitchen.

"My boiler will go out!" Irenka exclaimed merrily.

Her colleagues passed lengthy comments on her concerns.

Vladimir stayed silent so as not to overdose on oxygen.

Trakarova and Kilian were whirling round the dance floor.

"Ah, Baloo," whispered Beata. "Teach me the Master Words for this people."

She was already a bit tipsy.

2. Our departure from the school meant the parting of the ways for us.

Although I gave Beata my telephone number at the publishing house, she didn't call even once during the first month. I heard she had started going out with some fellow called Jakub from the Rainbow ecology movement, and apparently she had even started to become active in it.

I found it all quite hilarious.

I enthusiastically immersed myself in my new editorial role, never once ceasing to rejoice silently; only a few days before, I had been explaining possessive subordinate clauses *ad nauseam*, eating in the school canteen and quarrelling with Chvatalova-Sukova; now I was editing Ivan Klima, lunching at Manes with Pavel Kohout and discussing literature with Eva Kanturkova!

I couldn't welcome those changes enough.

I even flew to Germany.

A Czech teacher flying Lufthansa!

Beata - I must admit - seldom entered my mind. She was out of sight.

I was reminded of her indirectly, however, on two occasions.

Firstly, I learnt from Jaromir (and subsequently from the *Zbraslav News*) that she and several young fellows from the SOS Animals foundation had broken into the school and released all the Principal's nutrias.

And secondly, a young man who brought to the editorial offices his own verse collection, *Clenched Eyes*, turned out to have been a fellow student of hers at the Arts Faculty. I made him a coffee, and we were soon on first-name terms.

"How did you find her?" I enquired. "*On the whole*, I mean."

I explained my interest by saying I had taught her sister for several years. He shrugged:

"She was awfully *pretentious*," he recalled. "You know, the kind of girl who reads Joyce in the metro..."

I rather liked him.

But I didn't understand his poems.

It was not until the end of February, however, early one frosty evening after leaving work, that I eventually saw her in person. She was outside the K-Mart store demonstrating in favour of animal rights along with her friends from the SOS Animals movement.

Apart from Beata, eight or nine people were taking part in the demonstration. Their naked bodies were swathed in a long sheet with the slogans *A fur coat is the badge of the murderer! The skins keep you warm but your hearts are cold as ice!* and *Bare skins rather than animal skins!*

The passers-by found it all very amusing.

As did the two policemen present.

Beata shivered with the cold.

The sight of her naked shoulders filled me with an urge to give her a cuddle, but I couldn't even talk to her as my briefcase, shoes and gloves were made of leather.

So I headed for the metro.

Some time in mid-April, when she was looking for modelling clay in the city centre, she finally called in at the publishing office.

She was wearing an unbleached linen dress, unvarnished wooden beads and rope sandals, so she looked rather like something from the display window of the nearby craft shop.

In her hand she carried a little bamboo bird cage containing a sick thrush.

I mentioned catching sight of her at the demonstration.

She bade me to *kindly* bear in mind that it took 65 mink or 130 chinchillas to make a mink coat.

I rapidly changed the subject.

"You're looking well," I said.

She was very tanned for the time of year.

She told me she had spent two weeks on premature honeymoon with Jakub in the Brdy Hills. They had played lacrosse and baked pancakes on hot stones. They had cooked in a cow's stomach. She was now back in Prague, but Jakub had gone off into the forest for a few more days to sort out some personal problems.

I wasn't entirely new to this kind of thing so I didn't bat an eyelid, but my female colleagues in the office weren't able to suppress amiably bemused smiles.

Beata urged them *also* to try changing their life-styles as the tropical rain forests were disappearing at the rate of one soccer pitch per second and every single American produced more waste daily than he himself weighed.

· This anti-American barb even made me raise my eyebrows.

It must have registered with Beata too, as she immediately started to tell us how she had been demonstrating with the *organisation* outside McDonalds on Vodicka Street - the very place where she and Steve used to go at least once a week and where she had gotten to know the whole staff.

"They just couldn't understand...," Beata grinned. "You should have seen them!"

Her appealing self-mockery served to ease the tension in the publishing office, and we laughed along with her.

I never made Jakub's - or the Looney's - acquaintance. Logically it must have been one of the fellows in front of the K-Mart, but I still don't have a clue which one. He must have been a sensitive, unselfish sort though, one who was prepared to make personal sacrifices for the *movement*, because as soon as the news of all those massacred whales reached his ears, he cancelled the wedding and went off to Norway for a year.

3. *Yet deep within, my aunt and I were bothered and greatly disturbed by him, and I confess he is still to this very minute on my mind. I often dream of him at night, and the mere existence of such a man has had a thoroughly disturbing and disquieting effect on me, although I have come to like him.* Herman Hesse, *Steppenwolf.*

Another component of the Windows computer operating system, which - as I think I've mentioned - I'm using to write this book is a so-called *screen saver*. I can only describe its operation in layman's terms: If, after a certain specifiable period of time, you fail to touch the mouse or the keyboard, the text on the screen changes into an optional dark moving picture. As a result, it takes just three minutes of dreamy inaction in the case of my computer for a screen saver by the name of *Starfield Simulation* to pop up on my screen. I now end up gawping more and more frequently at a dark starry cosmos.

But she's nowhere there.

*Lost in desart wild
Is your little child.*

XII

1. After Steve and Jakub, the last of Beata's boyfriends was God. At first, though, it was not entirely clear *which one*.

First of all she got to know several Mormons from Smichov, but her objection to them (according to Agata) was that they professed polygamy and were Americans. She later came to hear about an ecological farm near Benesov run by members of the Hare Krishna movement, and for several days she toyed with the idea of going there; but apparently she was put off by the fact that they worked the whole day in the fields and had to get up early in the morning. She also used to frequent a certain evangelical minister in the southern suburbs, but it was too far to travel and the minister struck her as being complacent. Besides, each time she went, she was harassed by Romanies in the passage of the apartments where he lived (Agata described them as *Gypsies*, of course). I couldn't help smiling because Beata's search for God was rather reminiscent of our earlier search for furniture. Eventually, I discovered, Beata was won over by the Jehovah's Witnesses in Zbraslav - they were the nearest and cheapest and delivered God right to her door.

As you can tell, I belong to that numerous band of ignoramuses whose only conviction, perhaps, is that there is *something* that transcends us, though it doesn't necessarily have to be God (hence we are ironically dubbed *somethingists* by Father Halik). Only once in my life has God spoken to me personally, and that was in front of the display window at Bata's shoe store on Wenceslas Square, where, through the mediation of a little Pakistani boy in an orange T-shirt, He told me that He *truly loved* me (though at first I thought that this message somehow had something to do with the price of the men's lace-ups on display). Moreover, at the time I was hearing from Agata about Beata's conversion, I was editing Kohout's novel *I Am Snowing* and was unable to overcome a certain aversion towards women who endure painful heart-searching on a Sunday morning over whether they should go pray or go skating instead. I really have no wish to bring down on my head the wrath of the press officer of the relevant council of bishops or even the papal council for dialogue with unbelievers, but if I am to write *the truth*, my deepest feeling about Beata's final phase can best be described by the irreverent paraphrase *What man hath joined let not God put asunder*.

2. Rapid succession of chapters to increase tension.

The end is near. It has taken me around five months to get this far. For the first three months I wrote the first version during my evenings and weekends, and I wrote the second draft at one go in March and April. I just can't wait to bury Beata a few pages further on and then *knock off* at last.

The second - and last - letter that Kral sent me arrived at the beginning of July (at first I considered antedating the arrival of the letter for better effect, in order to have it arrive *a year and a day later* like in the fairy stories, but later it struck me as taking poetic licence a bit far, and I abandoned the idea). The tone of the letter was affable and spontaneous. Kral wrote that he was sorry he had not contacted me sooner *after all we went through together last year*. But he had had serious business worries, he said. Why don't I call round some time? He had heard I was spending July in Zbraslav and had the feeling that Beata *would rather like the idea. By the way*, she had taken up writing again. She had actually written something *quite long* but now that I was *so famous* she was too shy to show it to me. How about a repeat of last year's *successful* writing course? It was only *something that had just struck him at that moment*, but it might be worth considering. Wouldn't I like to drop by some time? Say next Friday? Around half past five? They were all *really looking forward* to seeing me.

3. *Story-telling as a weapon against cruel, senseless reality.*
Milan Jankovic

It was also obvious to me I had been in the bathroom too long.

My wife observed my preparations with a quizzical eye.

"Would you mind telling me where you're going?" she asked.

I informed her that I had an almost *physical* aversion to questions framed in that manner and asked her whether she might not avoid them in the future.

"Would you kindly stop lecturing me!" she demanded angrily.

The garden was in a state of neglect.

However conceited it may sound, Petrik seemed pleased to see me. He was wearing a Bart Simpson tie.

To my surprise he was on his own.

"Where's your buddy?"

"In the hospital," he smiled.

"Let me guess," I said. "Careless handling of his service revolver? Demolishing a load-bearing wall with a karate chop?"

"Nothing like that!" he laughed. "His appendix, that's all."

Agata, on the other hand, was in no laughing mood, and my disinclination to ask the reason made her even sulkier.

I ruffled her hair in a friendly fashion.

"Calm your hormones!" she said insolently.

And not without cause.

Kral was out playing tennis. Mrs Kralova looked harried. She wouldn't offer me coffee - apparently *the nun upstairs* was intending to make me one.

I consoled her in the words of Goethe: *However turbulent the juice is stirred, it will turn to wine in the end.*

"Let's hope so," she said sceptically.

And not without cause.

4. The staircase up to the attic was once more fear-ridden.

I was afraid of again entering a gloomy twilight and coming across deathly pale lips gibbering fanatical prayers - but instead I entered a sunny bedroom full of bright loud colours, as during Beata's American phase the original black/pink combination had not only been boldly supplemented by a number of purple and bright yellow accessories (mostly mobile), but in addition, the wardrobe, tables and the bookshelf had also been painted the same colours in the freest possible way. The new curtains were plum-coloured.

A small cross hung between two Andy Warhol posters.

"What were you expecting?" Beata smiled. "A noviciate's cell?"

She was looking well, but most of all I was pleased to find her capable of irony.

"Anything," I said candidly. "But most likely a refuge for lost thrushes. Or a screening plant for non-ecological waste..."

She gazed into my eyes with a strange kind of indulgent superiority.

I discovered a second little cross in the open neck of her lacrosse shirt.

I stood back slightly.

"I baked you a tart," she smiled hospitably.

She sprinkled coffee into the filter paper and switched on the coffee-maker.

The priest's housekeeper were the words that came to mind.

"You told me you felt like Mary Pickford in church," I reminded her. "Has something changed since, then?"

I just couldn't help it. My blood was boiling.

Faith is a gift, she said calmly. And she was convinced, she said, that one day I too would receive that gift, because I was a sensitive person, and besides, we were all building blocks in the edifice of which Christ was the cornerstone.

To hear the word *Christ* in that room... From those lips.

Relying on the scrappy knowledge I had gained from the Illustrated Children's Bible that someone gave my daughter for Christmas, I scornfully called into question all that *folklore*.

"Have some more tart," she urged me gently.

"You told me," I exploded, "that you could never ever convert because it would mean you becoming a *pupil* once more! You said you'd never put up with any teacher again!"

She said she hadn't become a pupil. She had become a branch of the tree that was Jesus.

She stroked my hand soothingly.

I gave up.

We then spent a very pleasant, Christian evening together. We talked about Agata, school, writing and book publishing.

When I came to leave, she let me kiss her on the cheek and went to make the sign of the cross on my forehead.

Her of all people!

I crossly grabbed her hand - admittedly she had done all sorts of things with my body in the past, but this was the limit.

She gave me a sympathetic look.

"Wait a moment," she said.

She went to fetch me a little blue hardback book, *Questions for Young People: Practical Answers*. She said she realised I would find the way it was written a bit off-putting, but it was the content, not the form, that mattered.

"You mustn't just read it like a pupil's composition," she laughed.

I turned up the contents page: *Why should I honour my father and my mother? Drugs and alcohol. How I can come closer to God.*

"The Little Red Book in blue," I commented.

A look of reproach in her eyes.

I promised her that I would read it as *impartially* as possible.

"God bless, then," I said.

Thus the last look she ever bestowed on me in her life was one of hurt feelings.

I can still picture it vividly.

A curious result of the increase of historical consciousness is that people think explanation is a necessity of survival. Saul Bellow

Contrary to my promise I didn't open *Questions for Young People* until I was making notes for this novel. I read among other things that *masturbation is an unclean habit, that too much alcohol is like a snake bite* and that *we can spend our free time healthily with some hobby.* Equally inspiring was the chapter dealing with literature: *Romantic novels can be thrilling. But do they provide a healthy outlook on life and marriage?*

5. A frightening experience (composition).

When we were coming home from Denmark, it took us a long time to come home because we were coming back across Germany, and in Germany they were always repairing the roads we were coming back on. It was late at night when we arrived home and something was in the letter-box, so I went for the key and when I opened the letter-box, I found out that my friend Beata was dead. The blood froze in my veins and the shock took my breath away.

Though assured by the Christian experts that *a personal friendship with God helps to overcome deep depression*, Beata had failed to overcome hers. Even though she was aware - if she had indeed read the manual - that *suicide is no solution*, she had gone ahead anyway. She hadn't gone out and bought herself something to cheer her up like Melanie, or planned a little outing like Debbie or cooked herself a favourite meal like Daphne, or even tried to do the crossword puzzles published in the *Awake!* magazine - no, instead, like Vivienne she just couldn't imagine that she would one day get over her depression, so she got in her black Golf and drove into a pillar of the bridge over the Strakonice road at a hundred and ten miles an hour.

183

And she never woke up again.

And the entire town was swathed in crepe.

And her heart, transformed to ash, was lifted in the palm of school caretaker Frantisek Nedelnicek and scattered in the wind above the meadows of the Garden of Remembrance, which is the pride of the citizens of Zbraslav.

I write a novel in order to preserve the living but also to lead out of oblivion the past and my own dead, to rescue myself from it. So long as I write, there remains a glimmer of hope for that return journey, that return to life and consciousness, to human will and a human face. Daniela Hodrova.

6. And yesterday I watched my daughter combing her hair in the front hall mirror.

She worked deftly like a grown-up woman.

She noticed me:

"What's the matter?" she asked with a timid smile, her hands behind her head and a hairclip in her mouth.

The little angel.

"Nothing."

I prodded her affectionately.

She lost her balance, and her hair fell from her clip.

"Calm your hormones!" she scowled.

The English writer Graham Greene was notorious, among other things, for his practice of using the last sentence of his books to raise doubts about everything he had asserted previously. In the case of the present novel, a *Greenian* ending might run as follows:

"You've *gone to town again*," said my wife ironically when she had finished reading the manuscript.

She probed me with her eyes, trying to judge from my guilty expression the extent and gravity of my sins. It meant, however, that she was only just making up her mind whether or not to be angry.

"Maybe you ought to have taken that job instead, though," she said pensively.

I wanted to hug her, but she pushed me away.

"Oh, come on," I said, reassuring her, "you mustn't take literature so seriously."

About the translators: A.G. Brain is the joint pen-name of the Anglo-Czech translating team of Gerry and Alice Turner, who made their name in the Seventies and Eighties as pseudonymous translators of writings by banned authors, notably, Vaclav Havel, Ivan Klima, Karel Pecka, Milan Simecka and Ludvik Vaculik. Their recent translations include Klima's novel *Judge on Trial* and the play *Between Dog and Wolf* by Daniela Fischerova.

The Turners are honorary members of the Czech Centre of International P.E.N. and live with their children in rural County Wexford, Ireland.